Praise for the Ava Logan Mystery Series

"Well-drawn characters, a dash of romance, and enough logically constructed red herrings to keep the reader guessing right up to the end distinguish this tightly woven tale."

— *Publishers Weekly*

"The first in Willis' planned series mixes murder and romance with enough suspects to keep you guessing."

— *Kirkus Reviews*

"As a reader who loves intricate mysteries that are filled to the brim with investigations, I'm grateful there will be more to come."

— *Suspense Magazine*

"A well-wrought tale of the secrets concealed beneath the surface of small-town Appalachia...Willis is a seasoned professional who gives us just enough red herrings to keep us guessing to the end."

— Margaret Maron,
New York Times Bestselling Author of *Long Upon the Land*

"A page-turning balance of small-town life and an unsolvable mystery with characters we wish we knew for real. *Tell Me No Lies* is a mystery that will not disappoint."

— C. Hope Clark,
Author of *Echoes of Edisto*

"Lynn Chandler Willis writes with a voice as big as the Appalachians. *Tell Me No Lies* is a compelling mystery and a spot-on depiction of newspapering in a small town. I'm already looking forward to more from Ava Logan."

— Brad Parks,
Shamus, Nero, and Lefty Award-Winning Author of *Say Nothing*

TELL
ME
YOU
LOVE
ME

The Ava Logan Mystery Series
by Lynn Chandler Willis

TELL ME NO LIES (#1)
TELL ME NO SECRETS (#2)
TELL ME YOU LOVE ME (#3)

TELL ME ME YOU LOVE ME

AN AVA LOGAN MYSTERY

LYNN CHANDLER WILLIS

HENERY PRESS

Copyright

TELL ME YOU LOVE ME
An Ava Logan Mystery
Part of the Henery Press Mystery Collection

First Edition | July 2019

Henery Press, LLC
www.henerypress.com

Trade Paperback ISBN-13: 978-1-63511-523-9
Digital epub ISBN-13: 978-1-63511-524-6
Kindle ISBN-13: 978-1-63511-525-3
Hardcover ISBN-13: 978-1-63511-526-0

Printed in the United States of America

For single moms and dads everywhere

ACKNOWLEDGMENTS

A big thanks to my conference roomie, Karen Fritz, and my friend, J.D. Allen for helping me get the terminology right. J.D. offered suggestions, which I took, and it made the story richer and stronger. To International Bestselling Author, Steve Berry, thank you for being so accessible and eager to help. You helped me shape the first chapter into something publishable. Thanks to Joe and Pam Hersh for sharing Tucker, the little beagle, with us. Yes, he and his little howl, was the inspiration for Tucker, the little beagle. Thanks to Mary Ann Yow, owner and director of Easter's Promise, for allowing me to use their name and purpose to help tell this story. If you're looking for a worthy cause to support, check them out at easterspromise.com.

CHAPTER 1

My body ached from shivering. Days like this made me wish I'd never started the newspaper. In the small town of Jackson Creek, the human-interest stories often outweighed the hard news. Today was one of those fluff pieces readers loved and I froze my ass off to get. Pudge Collins said something, but I wasn't sure I heard him right. What was missing? "One what?"

"Dog. One of the dogs is missing. Sounds like Tucker."

The pack of beagles bayed in hot pursuit of a fleeing cottontail. The ear-shattering wail echoed through the stillness and reverberated over the barren field. Pudge Collins stared across the cutover with his head cocked to one side. Listening. His breath rose and fell in a controlled manner. Calm. Steady. Carhartt coveralls stretched tight across his stout frame, partially camouflaged by his blaze orange vest. His eyes narrowed. Mouth drawn.

I concentrated to hear what Pudge heard, or didn't hear. Relentless barking in the distance and silence surrounding us. I surveyed the field trying to see what he saw. Dead of winter. Leafless trees allowing peeks into the thickets. Beyond, blue-tipped mountains rose behind the timbered field, towering over the forest. A sky full of grey clouds threatened snow and sleet.

Pudge brought his binoculars up to eye-level and studied the woods. I shivered against the bone-chilling cold despite my own briar-proof coveralls and down vest. My teeth chattered. "How do you know Tucker's missing?"

"The bark. You're a mother, Ava. You can probably pick your own kid's cry out of a crowd."

I could tell their laugh, their cough, and their cry, even in the midst of others. My son, Cole, was sixteen, tall and lanky with a voice that hadn't quite grown into the body. Daughter, Emma, was thirteen and more mature than me, and at two, my adopted daughter, Ivy, could go from a sweet angel full of kisses to a demon in a toddler's body within seconds. Like each one, their voices were individual. I doubted it was the same with dogs, but Pudge was the expert. Raising prize-winning, rabbit-hunting beagles was his claim to fame and the readers of the *Jackson Creek Chronicle* were going to learn everything there was to know about it.

I glared at the dingy clouds overhead now spitting sleet. Weather aside, and Pudge a man of few words, this interview was already challenging enough. "What do we do now?"

Pudge climbed down from his perch on the tree stump. Although he was in great shape for his age, Pudge was pushing seventy and I worried about his agility should the ground turn slippery. "We go looking for him."

"What about the other dogs?" I looked around the field. I heard them in the distance, but the only thing I could see were trees dead with winter chill.

"They'll circle back. Rabbits run in circles so they ain't going anywhere."

Although my legs had grown stiff from the freezing

temperature, I forced them to move and followed Pudge into the woods. Brambles snagged at my coveralls while I swatted tree branches out of the way. The dogs howled in the distance, minus the one rogue beagle, who, for whatever reason, had deserted its pack.

"What do you think happened to it?" I visualized a stalking bobcat and glanced cautiously around my surroundings. Certainly if the poor pup had fallen victim, we'd have heard the yelps. Bears were common in the high country part of North Carolina, but given the time of year, they were probably snug in a warm cave sleeping their way into spring. Which, at the moment, seemed enticing.

Pudge reminded me we were talking about a fifteen-pound beagle. "No telling what happened to him. Tucker has a mind of his own. I don't think he's gonna make much of a hunter."

As we moved deeper into the forest, the barking of the others faded into the distance. Pudge high-stepped over a fallen tree then turned to extend a helping hand. Once I was on the other side, he moved a finger to his chapped lips and whispered *shhhh*. He cocked his head again then tramped off to his left.

"Dang dog," he muttered.

He blended into the thicket with only glimpses of his orange vest visible. Fallen branches snapped and creaked under his heavy footfall. I stayed put and watched him from the short distance.

After a moment, he called back to me. "Found him."

My breath hitched as I imagined the dog gravely injured. But then Pudge shooed the beagle away with a voice edging on surprise. "*What the...*Tucker, get away from that."

The dog whined as Pudge shoved him away from whatever he'd found. I pushed through the bare branches of the non-evergreens while pine needles brushed against my wind-raw cheeks. The exact reason as an avid hiker that I stayed on the trail. Pudge whistled ominously at whatever it was Tucker had discovered. "Ava—you might want to come see this."

I quickened my step and stopped behind Pudge, peering around his shoulder. He had leashed the beagle, keeping the pawing dog close at hand. "Is that—"

"An arm. That's what it looks like to me." Pudge toed the nearby ground, exposing even more of the skeletal remains.

My cheeks flushed as searing warmth exploded throughout my body. What *were* we looking at? Sun-bleached and weather worn, the bones had been here awhile. Dirt clung to them as if it was a part of the DNA.

I wanted to lie and tell Pudge the bones were probably nothing. Could have been an accident that happened ages ago; this was old mill property. But I'd never been a good liar, even with sleet now pinging off the trees and that rush of heat I'd felt seconds ago now gone.

People didn't just lose an arm or leg and have it go unnoticed. Not around here. Jackson Creek, North Carolina sat nestled in the heart of Appalachia. The small town was as old as the mountains surrounding it; the legends ran as deep as the valleys.

I ran through a mental list of folks in the area I knew had undergone an amputation. Being the town's newspaper owner, I knew most everyone in these parts—their diseases, their accidents, and the veterans who had given parts of themselves. The ones who lived before my thirty-five years, I knew their history. Yet, nothing sparked a memory.

Tucker tugged at the leash enough to move away a few feet. He dug at the ground in a frenzy, sending bits of earth scattering. Before Pudge pulled him back, the dog uncovered what looked like another bone. I quickly moved around Pudge and pushed Tucker aside. Thoughts crashed through my brain like colliding trains.

"Oh my God," I whispered.

"What is it?" Pudge pulled Tucker back and tightened his grip on the leash.

"It's a skull."

With a gaping bullet hole.

Jackson County Sheriff Grayson Ridge crouched beside the skeletal remains and used his gloved hand to gently sweep away accumulating snow. The county medical examiner, Bosher Garrett, stooped across from him and pointed toward what looked like an arm bone. The man had seen enough death, the memories were seared into his brain.

I watched from a few feet away, anxious to hear Bosher's speculation. At this stage that's all it would be.

A crew from the sheriff's department waited for direction from their boss. Grayson Ridge was in his second term as sheriff of Jackson County. At thirty-eight, he was young for the job and popular with the voters. He'd even won over the old-timers who liked their sheriffs with some age and seasoning. He'd been my dead husband Tommy's partner before he was killed in the line of duty. Grayson and I had history. We had a past, a present, and maybe even a future.

Grayson stood and brushed snow from the knees of his jeans. Snow clung to his dark hair, dampening it to a shine. "Let's get the tent set up. Protect as much of the area as possible."

Two of the techs hurried through the woods back to their vehicles to retrieve the tent, a purchase Grayson fought for when the county alderman cut the department's budget. In an area where the weather was prone to change from hour-to-hour, the tent served its purpose well.

Bosher pushed aside debris around the bones. "There doesn't appear to be any saw marks so it could have been torn away from the body, or probably just fell away from decay."

"A bear, maybe?" One of the deputies asked.

"Not unless the bear carries a gun," Grayson said with a nip of attitude. "You do see the bullet wound, right?"

My own cheeks flushed with embarrassment for the guy. It wasn't like Grayson to be snippy with anyone.

Bosher pointed at marks on the largest bone. "There are some teeth marks but they're not big enough to be a bear."

Probably Tucker, the wayward beagle.

Bosher stood and wobbled a bit on creaking knees. Approaching retirement, his own bones creaked and popped with every move. "Doctor Felicia Scranton runs a top-notch anthropology department at the university. This would be right up her alley."

"I've worked with her before. I'll give her a call," Grayson said. "Right now, let's collect what we can then lock it down under the tent."

The techs got busy putting what little evidence there was into bags. One sifted through the dirt with a hand trowel while another carefully bagged the bones. One documented the scene on camera.

Bosher scanned the woods, his well-lined face scrunched with questions. "And what were you doing up here again?" He looked at me with one bushy eyebrow raised.

"I'm doing a feature story on Pudge Collins and his beagles. The science behind rabbit hunting."

It sounded silly when I said it out loud. But the paper's readers loved the feature stories. They loved reading about their neighbors and their interests and hobbies. As much as I griped about being out here, rabbit hunting with prize-winning beagles would make a decent story. It would have to take a backseat for now, though. Skeletal remains had pushed it off the editorial calendar.

"You can't hunt rabbit with dogs in the snow. They can't pick up the right scent," Bosher said, his manner beyond condescending. "Any decent rabbit hunter would know that."

Bosher's and Pudge Collins' dislike for one another was legendary in these hills. It dated back to high school and a girl with a bee-hive hairdo. In the end, Ginny Turner chose Pudge. Three kids, six grandkids, and a revolving pack of beagles later, they were still married and happy, and Bosher still stewed.

"It wasn't snowing when we started." I wrapped my arms around myself and envied Pudge, now home and warm.

With the big bone safely bagged, the tech added a few scoops of the surrounding dirt. He jerked his hand back when the trowel picked up something shiny. "Hey, Sheriff, look at this."

He shook out the dirt, leaving a gold class ring exposed. The styling was old school with a large stone and thick band.

Grayson picked up the ring with his gloved-hand. "Jackson Creek High School. Class of 1967."

I said, "Anything ese?"

He looked on the inside of the band. "Initials KJD and MAM."

I jotted the initials and the date on my notepad then slipped the pad back into the pocket of my coveralls. Bosher held his hand out for the ring. After Grayson dropped it in his hand, he studied it hard as if it brought back memories. "1967. Two years ahead of me."

"Judging by the size of it, it's definitely a guy's ring," Grayson said.

"Which means the victim is a male?" the rookie deputy said.

Bosher dropped the ring in the evidence bag. "Not necessarily. Back then it was standard for a guy to give his class ring to his sweetheart. She'd wrap tape around the bottom to make it fit."

I wondered if Bosher had given Ginny Turner his class ring? I pushed aside the thoughts of Bosher's love triangle and concentrated on the sweethearts symbolized on the ring. KJD and MAM. It wasn't much, but it was a starting point.

CHAPTER 2

Finding skeletal remains was problematic in itself but finding them in the middle of a weather event amped up the challenge. Grayson surveyed the crime scene with a look of dread. Snow collected on his coat, having bypassed the flurry stage and was now falling hard. He glared at the skull with a weary look. The same weariness we all felt. "Anyone have an updated weather forecast?"

One of the techs shielded his phone from the snow. "Winter storm warning. Eight to ten inches. Current temp twenty-six degrees." The speed he was able to pull up that information told me he wasn't happy about being out here and was looking for a good excuse to head for warmth.

Grayson huffed out loud, turned up the collar of his coat and mumbled, "Damn. Where are they with that tent?"

The little beagle who couldn't sniff out a rabbit, had led us to what appeared to be a suicide or a murder. Either way, it was a skull with a bullet wound.

Bosher lifted the skull for a closer look. He handed it back to the tech who had uncovered it. "I can't tell for sure but the slug looks like a .22. No exit wound."

"Any idea how long it's been out here?" I asked, knowing it was a long shot. Until Bosher or the archeologist, Dr. Scranton, could do a full examination of what we had, the only thing we knew for sure was this person was alive in 1967.

Bosher looked around like the woods held the answer. Maybe they did. "When'd they shut down the mill?"

"July 3, 1988," Grayson answered quickly then looked back and forth between me and Bosher. Aware we wondered how he knew the exact date, he added. "My daddy worked there."

Why didn't I know that? "I thought he dug coal."

"He did. After the mill shut down." Grayson walked over to the crime scene photographer and told her something.

I got the feeling whatever it was he told her wasn't as important as putting an end to our conversation. Something was up with him but I couldn't put my finger on it. A wind gust pushed the thought of secrets to the back of my mind. I buried my face in my shoulder. My cheeks were raw enough from the cold.

The deputies finally returned with the tent, their breath coming in visible puffs.

Within minutes, they had the tent set up, covering the area where the remains had been found.

Was there a whole person buried within a certain square yardage of the woods? Or had animals scattered the remains?

The only thing I knew for sure was I'd taken all I could of the weather. I longed for a steaming cup of coffee and warm air. "What's next?" I asked whoever would answer.

Grayson scanned the area. "Collect as much as we can then zip up the tent and go home for the night."

Bosher nodded his agreement. "Sounds like a plan."

The deputy who couldn't see the bullet hole said, "I guess

we have a *really cold* case."

No one laughed. Any other time, I would have at least chuckled. The poor deputy was struggling to fit in but making an ass of himself while doing it.

After collecting as much evidence as possible, they secured the scene and we trudged back to our cars. I hung back at Grayson's Expedition, waiting for the others to pull away. With just the two of us left, I reached out and touched his face. "You okay?"

He smiled, pulling me to him. "I'm fine."

I cocked my head and grinned. "No, you're not. But I won't push. I'll see you later," I gave him a quick kiss then climbed into my Tahoe. He watched me, smiling, and I felt a little better. A little more at ease. Still, there was something bothering him and I hoped he trusted me enough to open up.

On my way back into town, I swung by Jackson Creek High School. They'd already dismissed school because of the road conditions but the office was still open. I sat in the parking lot and called Cole to make sure he made it home okay.

"I did donuts in the parking lot," he said, the pride filtering through his voice.

I stared at the tire-created donuts in the snow-covered parking lot. Looked like every kid at the school with a vehicle had the same fun. "You better be kidding."

"I am. Emma would have had a heart attack."

No, truth was Emma would have killed him for scaring her *then* had a heart attack. Either way, they were safe at home. Ivy was at Doretha Andrew's, my former foster-mother and pastor at the All Faith's Missionary Church. Doretha had raised me; I trusted her to babysit Ivy.

I made a dash to the covered walkway then rang the bell at

the school's main door. After a few seconds, the lock buzzed followed by a click. Being the owner of the local newspaper had its perks. I rarely had to show ID.

Warmth wrapped around me like a welcome blanket. I stamped the snow from my boots on the rubber mat then went to the office. Susan Joyner, the school secretary, looked up from a stack of papers and grinned.

"I'm not even going to ask about the coveralls."

"In my defense, it involves Pudge Collins."

She got a good chuckle out of that. "You were rabbit hunting."

"Tried to. The weather didn't cooperate." There was no need to go into detail about the remains found in the woods. Everyone in Jackson Creek would know soon enough as word tended to spread in towns like this.

"Where would I find a copy of the yearbook for the class of 1967?"

Susan exhaled a low whistle. "That's an old one. I'm pretty sure the library has every year, though."

I thanked her then walked down the main hall, taking a left after the cafeteria. I'd graduated from this school almost twenty years ago, but still remembered all its details—the metal lockers with their combination locks, the glass cases with decades of trophies, the hallways that held the voices of kids stuck in the middle. Not quite adults, no longer children.

Locker 214. Tommy kissed me for the first time right there. I stopped and ran my finger along the number plate, tracing the two then the one and finally, the four. There was a time, I supposed, that I did love him. Before he started using me as his personal punching bag.

I jerked my hand away from the locker as if it had thrown a

charge. Maybe it had. I thought about the class ring and the initials. What was KJD's story? Did he love MAM? Did she love him? I would need names before I could tell where their story went.

I hurried on down the hallway to the library. Martha Edmunson had been the librarian during my senior year. And now here she stood like no one had ever flipped the page on the calendar. The library had been upgraded but Martha held tight to another decade. Glasses too big for her face, a hairstyle from an eighty's sitcom, and too much eyeshadow almost struck a pity chord.

She put a stack of books on the rolling cart then looked me up and down. I knew by her expression she wondered about the coveralls. "Ava Logan. I don't think I've seen you this year. You missed the book fair."

The dig went in one ear and out the other. I do remember mentioning it in the school events column. "Susan said y'all had old copies of yearbooks in the library."

"We do. What year are you looking for?"

"1967."

She disappeared into a back room then returned a moment later with the book. "You must be hot on the trail of a good story."

Possibly. It was too soon to give out details. "Do you mind if I take it with me?"

Martha stared with a side-eye glance. "It's a research book. We don't check those out."

"I know, Martha. But this is important. I would appreciate it if you could make an exception just this once." I felt like I was groveling, and I hated groveling.

Martha's lips puckered into a tight knot of negativity. The

pucker morphed into a smirk. "Maybe you could mention something about the Methodist ladies' chicken-pot-pie sale in the paper."

I could spare the space in the community calendar more than I could do without the book. "Email me the details."

She reluctantly handed me the book with narrowed eyes and raised brows. "And this is just between us, right? I could get in trouble for this, you know."

Get in trouble with whom? She was the head librarian. I didn't question her and agreed. "Of course. No one will know."

"Good. Now if you'll excuse me, I need to get these put away so I can get out of here. I heard it's getting nasty out there."

I told her to drive safely then hurried out to my Tahoe. Skiers and slope owners were the only ones who would be happy about this weather. I turned the heat and fan up so the hot air would blow hard and fast. The wipers barely kept up with the white stuff splattering against the windshield.

While I waited for the defroster to kick in, I flipped through the yearbook. The senior class was in the front. Back then, the senior class pictures were taken in graduation robes and caps with tassels. None of the scenic, natural backgrounds like those of today. I quickly scanned some of the names and looked for initials corresponding to KJD. The names were listed alphabetically with two pages of last names beginning with D. Faces with uncertain futures stared back at me. The wipers slapping against the windshield jerked me out of 1967 and back to reality.

I laid the book in the passenger seat and headed to the office.

After standing in the sleet and snow half the day, being in a warm office would be a welcome change. I'd never been one for a typical desk job and the *Jackson Creek Chronicle* afforded me the freedom to work at my desk or be out and about. We were a small office and small operation with five regular staff members who managed to put a broadsheet newspaper out once a week.

The office was in an old mercantile shop on Main Street in Jackson Creek. Open and airy, we had desks, not cubicles, an old storage room converted into a break room, and a small office that I never used. Original plank flooring and a century-old wood stove reminded me daily of simpler times. Like when teenagers exchanged class rings. Now, class rings didn't even have the school colors.

I hurried into the office and stamped the snow from my boots. The office manager, Nola, gave me a second glance then burst out laughing. "Ain't you a sight in your coveralls and vest."

Well-kept and closer to retirement than she'd ever admit, Nola spewed Southern charm while running the office like a dictator.

I shrugged out of the vest and hung it on the coat tree to dry. "Rabbit hunting with Pudge Collins."

"Please tell me it was for a feature story."

"Well, it started out that way. Ended up being the discovery of skeletal remains with a bullet in the skull."

Nola's eyes widened. "Oh my."

The chatter in the office ceased as all eyes turned to me, including our guest in the waiting area.

He offered a hesitant smile along with a tiny wave. Late twenties, sandy blond hair, well-dressed in a navy sweater and dark jeans. Handsome in an L.L. Bean kind of way.

Nola cleared her throat then offered, "This is Aaron Bell. He's a documentary filmmaker and would like to speak with you a moment."

Documentary filmmaker. My guard sprang up immediately as the mere words made me uneasy.

Bell dug a business card from a leather case tucked into his back pocket. "I promise I won't take up much of your time."

I took the card and laid it on Nola's desk then shimmied out of the coveralls. I gave the card another look then carried it with me to the wood stove. *Aaron Bell, Documentary Filmmaker.* A Washington D.C. address and phone number. "If you don't mind chatting around the campfire, come on back."

Stripped down to jeans, a cable-knit sweater and wool socks, I hurried to the heat source. I backed up to it, allowing the warmth to penetrate the backside of my jeans.

I turned around when Bell joined me, standing on the other side of the stove. "It's wicked cold out there. I hope you weren't out in it too long."

"Long enough. How can I help you, Mr. Bell?"

"I'm doing a film on Appalachian culture and would like your help."

Another documentary on Appalachia. I studied him, trying to detect a questionable motive. "It's not a very original idea."

"My vision is."

Maybe it was his confidence, or the sincerity in his eyes, but his reply grabbed my attention. "And what is your vision, Mr. Bell?"

"Please, call me Aaron. There's a lot of good in this area. I want to show that to the outside world."

Although his face was warm with empathy, my suspicion rose. There had been dozens of films made about Appalachia and very few of them shed a good light on the area. "Look...*Aaron*, there is a lot of good in this area. But my experience is it tends to get overlooked when the camera starts rolling. I don't want be a part of that."

"Exactly why I need *you*. Who knows this area better than the newspaper publisher?"

I did know the area. The good and the bad. The joblessness, the meth and opioid problems, and the poverty and how it all blended together like a recipe for disaster. Beneath the ugly lay close-knit people who found ways to thrive despite their hardships, caring people who looked out for each other, and who viewed strangers with a wary eye.

With the chill from the outside world gone, I went to my desk and pushed the guest chair out as an invitation to Aaron. I'd listen to what he had to say before sending him on his way.

He immediately pulled the chair closer to me. "Look, I know you don't know anything about me, so I get your hesitation—"

"It has nothing to do with you personally. The people of this region trust me and I won't betray that trust."

He leaned forward, elbows on his knees. "I get it. I really do. It's not my intention to hurt anyone or make them look bad."

I heaved a weary sigh. *Hillbilly.* That's what I heard, although that wasn't what he had said. The people of Appalachia had been misrepresented more times than they'd been portrayed in a positive way. "Everyone starts with good intentions. But it doesn't always end that way."

"Then who better to keep us on track than someone who appreciates the people and their integrity?"

I knew nothing about this guy and wasn't falling for his flattery. Too much was at stake. "Look—"

"Look at some of my work. Google me. I'm not out to expose anyone or anything. There's enough darkness in the world. My vision is to show the good."

Despite my brain wanting to tell him no, my ears were listening. "Give me a few days to take a look. I've got a story that's going to take precedence right now, but I'll call you either way."

"Do you think it was murder?"

"What was murder?"

"The skull with a bullet."

My stomach sank with the possibility, or more likely, the reality. Still, I wasn't going to speculate with a total stranger. "We don't know that yet. Honestly, we're not even sure the remains are human."

"I've heard of cases like that where you can't really tell the species just by looking at it."

Maybe I was just tired, but the conversation couldn't end fast enough. "We all have ribs. I'll be in touch in a few days."

He flinched at the abruptness. "Sure. I'll ah...just wait for your call. I'm staying in Boone through the weekend. Just take a look at some of my work. I think you'll see I'm a man of my word."

Bell wasn't even out the door before the buzz started in the office.

Nola sprang up while Quinn Carter spun his chair around and rolled over to my desk. With his eyes narrowed, he threw me a suspicious look. "You are going to do it, aren't you?"

If anyone should be in front of a camera, it was Quinn. He had the rugged handsomeness of a veteran war correspondent although he was barely thirty. No one knew his whole story so I had yet to piece the puzzle together of why he was here. He had the looks and the nose for news that could carry him places in the broadcasting world, yet he squeaked by on what I could pay him and seemed happy at our weekly paper.

"This area doesn't need another documentary on it. So, probably not."

Nola crossed her arms and twisted her mouth like she'd already decided for me. "But you know he does have a point. No one knows this area better than you do."

"The university is full of professors who've made a career out of Appalachian studies. I am by no means an authority."

"No, but you're the heart and soul."

Ever the newshound, Quinn moved on. "What's this about skeletal remains?"

I filled them in on what I knew, which truthfully wasn't much. "Grayson is going to call an anthropology professor from the university to help with the recovery."

"Could you really not tell if it's human?" Nola asked.

"It's human. With a gunshot wound in the skull. I wasn't going to say that with a filmmaker sitting right here, though."

"Are they thinking murder?" Quinn frowned.

I touched the side of my head. "Either that or self-inflicted."

An incoming call pulled Nola back to her desk. Quinn asked, "Were there other bones around it or was it just the skull?"

"There were others. One looked like a tibia, maybe some fingers."

"Any idea how long it's been there?"

"No way to tell at this point. But there was a class ring from 1967 found with some of the bones."

Quinn's gaze focused on me, his eyes wide. He had that look of surprise a news person gets when a puzzle is coming together. "*Damn.* You think they've been out there that long?"

I felt the same impatience he felt. "We won't know until the professor can examine the remains, and even then it'll be her best guess. Besides, just because the ring was from a class that graduated decades ago, doesn't mean the person's been dead that long. Decay is actually a pretty fast process."

Nola hung up the phone and turned around in her chair to face me. "Can we stop talking about decaying bodies and worry about those roads out there? The snow's piling up."

Out the front window, wind blew the falling snow sideways. It was already a couple inches deep. The roads would be impassable sooner than later. "How are we on production?"

"On schedule." There was a reason Nola was the office manager. She oversaw every aspect of the paper and kept us all on track.

"Are you going to run anything about the remains?" Quinn asked.

"Yeah, I'm going to write it now. I'll just cover the basics and go in depth when we know more."

The layout manager, Danny Olson, turned away from the double monitor Mac in the corner and threw a harsh glare at me. "So you want me to kill the town council?"

Quinn burst out laughing. "Yes, please. And painfully."

"I meant the article," Danny said, unamused.

I melted into the chair, trying to make myself as small as possible. "Sorry, Danny. You don't need to make that much space because we don't know a lot yet. I do have pictures if we need to fill."

He grumbled and turned back to the computer where he worked his magic.

"The roads?" Nola hinted.

"Change the phone message to say we're closing early due to the weather. Y'all go on and get out of here before it gets worse."

Within minutes, the office was officially closed and most of the staff headed home. I stayed to write the article on the remains found and Danny stayed to place it. I uploaded three pictures and a headline: "Human Remains Found Near Old Mill."

Peering over Danny's shoulder while he worked his magic, the story came to life. I pointed to the picture of the skull, the bullet hole concealed. I knew better than to reveal a key piece of evidence. "Let's move that up under the headline."

He bumped down the article to two columns wide then brought the picture up beside the lead. "What do you think?" he asked.

"That's an attention getter. Let's get out of here before the roads get any worse."

After we closed up, I called Doretha to ask her to have Ivy ready to go then carefully navigated the road through town. Main Street ran two miles through the heart of Jackson Creek. Not all, but most of the town's businesses fell somewhere within those two miles. A mom-and-pop dime store, where you could still buy candy by the pound from a wooden barrel and a soda in a glass bottle with a metal cap, sat beside a jewelry store. A clothing store where you could buy vintage or current fashion alongside novelty t-shirts and sweatshirts with *I love North Carolina* logos, the word "love" replaced with a red heart, shared an awning with the hardware store. A couple of trendy, artsy-type shops appealed to the money-spending tourists as much as the mom-and-pop stores. What townsfolk considered a way of life, visitors found charming.

Now wasn't the time for tourists or visitors other than skiers. Even the locals hid inside from bad bouts of winter weather. As I turned off of Main Street onto the side street, the

back tires pulled to the left, spinning in fresh fallen snow. I
carefully straightened the wheel, barely avoiding the ditch in
front of All Faiths Missionary Church. The small, white-washed
building with stain-glass windows had welcomed the lost for as
long as I could remember. Reverend Doretha Andrews had led
the soul-saving charge since the church's birth.

Doretha saved souls in the tiny church, and beside it, she
saved kids in her Civil War era home. She'd taken me when I
was eight years old, after my mother went to prison for killing
my abusive father. Doretha was a big-bosomed black lady with
swinging braids and a booming voice. She was also the anchor
that kept this skinny little white girl grounded.

At Doretha's, I left the Tahoe running so it wouldn't lose its
warmth and dashed inside. She'd anticipated wet shoes tracking
in snow and had already spread a couple towels on the floor in
the entryway. Just like she used to do when I was a kid.

I stood on one of the towels and called for Ivy. Doretha
poked her head around the corner from the kitchen. "Hey, Baby
Doll," she said, calling me by the name she'd given me years ago.
"I've got her ready to go."

Doretha disappeared for a moment then returned with Ivy
in tow. A head full of blonde curls framed an angelic face.
Emerald-colored eyes smiled back at me. Doretha had already
dressed her in her snowsuit, giving her a laugh-worthy waddle. I
picked her up and kissed her chubby cheeks.

Ivy wasn't mine by birth but I wasn't Doretha's by birth,
either. Ivy's mother had been a single mom and good friend who
met a tragic end. Doretha didn't have room for another foster
and I didn't want Ivy to be bounced around in the system. Cole
and Emma got a little sister and I got a toddler.

Doretha draped Ivy's bag over my shoulder. "Roads bad?"

"They're getting that way. I'll call you later and let you know if I'm going to open the office tomorrow." I started out the door, shuffling my feet carefully over the icy steps.

"Ain't no news worth dying over." She winked and her whole dimpled cheek rose.

Then it dawned on me. I called back from the driveway, "Didn't your brother work at the paper mill?"

"Calvin? He swept the floors if I remember right."

I wondered if KJD worked at the mill, too, or if he just had the bad luck to die there?

CHAPTER 3

The tracks in our driveway from Cole's truck were almost covered over with snow. I followed the faint tire path down the quarter-mile drive. It ended at the covered side porch of the farm house Tommy and I bought when Cole was a newborn. We had renovated the house ourselves. His sudden death on the day he failed to wear his kevlar vest left some of the house, much like our marriage, unfinished.

He robbed me of the joy of leaving him. Truth be told, my heart left him the first time he hit me.

The backdoor swung open, allowing Finn, our Border Collie, to rush outside. She barreled down the steps and danced around the yard joyously kicking up snow. Emma stood in the doorway, illuminated by the kitchen light.

"Need any help?" she asked.

I tossed her Ivy's bag and my purse then wrangled the tot from her car seat. With Ivy propped on my hip, I carried her and the Jackson Creek yearbook inside. Finn continued running circles in the yard until I called her in.

Emma stripped Ivy out of her snowsuit. It was much easier getting her out than in. If Doretha was my anchor, Emma was my compass. Smart with a developing sense of sass, she fluttered between mythical fairy and red-headed fireball.

She could also talk until your eyes glazed over. "Miss Myers said we probably wouldn't have school tomorrow because of the roads. If we don't, can I go to Doretha's and help with Ivy? I don't want to stay home all day with Cole."

"We'll see. If the roads are bad, I'll work from home so you can help me here with Ivy. How's that?"

It didn't ignite the same passion as the opportunity to go to Doretha's. I changed the subject. "Will you feed Finn and Boone, please." Boone, a domestic shorthair I had taken in, was seldom seen.

"This early?"

I jerked around to look at the clock on the microwave. 3:20. Maybe because I'd spent most of the day freezing in the woods, I'd lost track of time. "Yeah, okay. You can wait awhile. Mind entertaining Ivy while I get some work done?"

"Sure."

I fixed myself a cup of coffee then carried it and the yearbook into the sunroom. My sanctuary. Cloud soft leather furniture, a rock fireplace, with a wall of windows overlooking the river the town was named after.

After starting a fire, I opened all the curtains covering the floor-to-ceiling windows for a panoramic view of the falling snow. The swings of Ivy's playset in the backyard had collected several inches of the white stuff. Trees, normally bare this time of year, sparkled with ice crystals and thin layers of snow clung to branches. From this view, the winter weather was not only tolerable, but stunningly beautiful.

I took a notepad and pen from the side table drawer then curled up on the sofa in search of KJD.

Kelvin John Dennis played quarterback for the football team, center for the basketball team and pitched for the baseball team. If he'd lettered in sports, wouldn't that have been symbolized on the ring somewhere? Blond hair cut neatly. Perfect smile. I jotted his name down and his senior stats.

Karl Jeffery Daniels, class president, president of the Beta Club and the Junior Civitans. A pleasant smile. Solid. I bet he went on to law school. Keith Jessup Davis, no senior stats, only one picture in the whole book. Dark, sad eyes. Did not want to be there. I doubted he'd have bought a class ring. Still, I wrote down his name.

Kenneth James Dupree, average looking guy, dark wavy hair, hooded eyes. I'd seen the eyes before but couldn't place them. No clubs, no sports. But he didn't look angry like Keith Davis. Just an average guy. I could see him standing at a grill in a backyard, small paunch of a belly. Wife inside the three bedroom, two-bath house making potato salad.

I scanned through the rest of the Ds, looking for girls with those initials. There was one: Kimberly Jean Douglas.

She was gorgeous. A cheerleader, President of the Home Ec club, member of the Honor Society. Like Kenneth Dupree, I could see her married, three kids, head of the PTA. If she'd lived long enough to get married and have children.

Were one of these *the* KJD? What was the story behind the death? I retrieved the laptop from the upstairs bedroom to dig further into what these guys did after graduation. Once I got back to the sunroom, Emma and Ivy were coloring pictures of unicorns at Ivy's little play table. Finn followed me back to the sofa then curled up at my feet.

About a half hour on research into Kelvin Dennis' past and present, Grayson called. I snatched up the phone, ready to hear his voice. "Hey."

"Hey. Did you get warm?"

"I'm thawing out. You?"

"Just got back to the office. Had a domestic disturbance we had to settle."

A sudden twinge of guilt seeped through my warm and comfortable bones. Poor guy'd been out in this shit all day. "Maybe I can warm you up tonight."

"*Hmmm.*"

I envisioned the corner of his lip turning up in his devilish grin. He sounded better than he had at the scene. "I love you."

"Love you, too. Dr. Scranton's coming up tomorrow."

I straightened on the sofa. "So soon?"

"She doesn't have a class tomorrow. It just worked out that way."

"I would like to do a profile piece on her." It beat the hell out of a pack of beagles.

He laughed. "I thought so. We're planning on heading to the scene around nine if you wanted to be there."

Being invited to a crime scene by the top lawman in the county wasn't a perk of sleeping with the sheriff that I took lightly. We still had professional lines we didn't cross. "I'll be there."

"She's one of the best there is. We're lucky she's close by. It'll be interesting to see what she comes up with." He sounded tired. Beat, as a matter of fact.

"Any ideas for supper?" Not that I wanted to spend a great deal of time in the kitchen, but I'd feed him a warm meal if he wanted it.

"Not really. Y'all go ahead. I'll be awhile in the office."

We chatted for a few more minutes about nothing in

particular while Kelvin Dennis glared at me from his mug shot. He was arrested in '73 for possession of stolen property. Paid his debt to society by working at the community center. Arrested again in '78 for assault and battery. Charges dropped.

Grayson cleared his throat. "Hello? You still there?"

I snapped back to the conversation. "Yeah. I'm sorry. I'm looking through the yearbook from 1967 and have the initials narrowed down to five. Four guys and one girl. One of them has a record."

"In Jackson County?"

"Yeah."

"Interesting. Hopefully Dr. Scranton can give us a timeline before too long. At least then we'll know what year we're looking at."

"True." The only thing we knew for sure was the victim was alive in 1967.

He sighed heavily. "I'm going to get some stuff together for tomorrow, then I'll be on home."

Home. Grayson hadn't officially moved in but slept at my house almost every night. He even had a couple drawers and a corner of the closet for his clothes. Plus, his toothbrush, razor, and shampoo were in the bathroom.

"Okay. Love you. And be careful." I clicked off my phone then pushed aside the warm fuzzies and dove back into matching the past with the present.

Kelvin Dennis was arrested again in 1983, again for assault and battery. Charges were dismissed, again. Beating up on someone followed by dropped charges looked like domestic violence to me. A tearful promise of never hitting you again followed by a declaration of loving you forever equaled an emotional bribe to tell the judge it was all a misunderstanding.

Rinse, repeat.

Bastard.

Only it looked like he never did repeat the process again, or she stopped reporting it.

I did a search of obituaries for Kelvin John Dennis and found a few scattered across the country, but none matching the age range. Recent Jackson County tax records showed a house and property belonging to Kelvin and Shelly Dennis on Fisher Road. I noted the address. Broadening the search for public records, I scanned the marriage licenses and divorces. They exchanged vows June 23, 1969. For better or for worse. Through a slap here, a kick there. Happily ever after.

A bitter taste crept up my throat, driving away my interest in KJD. I hated to admit it, but if the remains were Kelvin's, I'd struggle to call him a victim. I moved on to Karl Jeffery Daniels.

His name produced several links and websites. Many were associated with Franklin, Abrams, and Daniels law firm. I smiled, knowing I'd guessed right about the former class president. Since he was still very much alive, I checked him off and changed focus to the next one on the list.

Keith Jessup Davis, the one with the sad eyes, died in Vietnam. Like his picture in the yearbook, little fanfare surrounded his life and death. I stared at the three entries with sympathy. He *did* matter. Even if his digital footprints said otherwise. Guilt fluttered in my gut when I erased his name from the search bar and typed in the next one, and the last guy. Kenneth James Dupree.

A spattering of links popped up with different variations of the name. I narrowed it down to two: an article from a newspaper in Knoxville, Tennessee dated 1969, and an obituary listing him as a relative. I opened the obituary first. It, too, was datelined Knoxville. Victor Cecil Dupree died August 4, 1986 and was survived by his wife Katherine, three children and two siblings. He was preceded in death by son Kenneth J. Dupree. I went back to the article from 1971. A headline below the fold read: "Family Wants Answers for MIA Son."

Victor and Katherine Dupree will take their questions all the way to the State Department if need be to find the truth about their son's disappearance. According to the Duprees, their son, Kenneth, 20, was discharged from the army in June but that's all they know.

After two tours in Vietnam, Kenneth notified his parents three months ago his duty was up. Kenneth never returned home and his parents lost touch. Victor Dupree says he was told by the army that his son probably "stayed" in Southeast Asia.

I stopped reading. If the Duprees were from Knoxville, then *that* Kenneth James Dupree probably wasn't the one who graduated from Jackson Creek High School. That left Kelvin Dennis and Kimberly Douglas. Statistically, a woman's not going to commit suicide with a gun. But what if it wasn't suicide?

I did a search for *Kimberly Jean Douglas* and came up with far fewer entries than I'd expected. She'd married Michael Andrew Morris in 1969, divorced him in 1970, then seemed to fall off the face of the earth.

There it was. All the initials. KJD and MAM. I quickly flipped to the last names beginning with "M" and Michael Morris offered a sweet smile. Looked like your average guy. He didn't look like Class President material but he wasn't the bottom of the barrel either.

Finn nudged my hand, jostling the laptop. It was only then I realized I'd spent way too much time chasing a ghost we hadn't yet confirmed existed. Finn reminded me she couldn't feed herself. Neither could the kids. Not decently, anyway.

I shut down the laptop then followed the hungry dog into the kitchen. Boone appeared from nowhere and mewed, curling around my feet. There were days I wondered if they really loved me, but I never doubted they needed me. After filling both their bowls, I had just started supper when Cole and his *girlfriend* Paisley came from upstairs and stood at the counter like it was something they did every day.

Slack-jawed, my eyes wouldn't blink. Not that I didn't like Paisley, because I did. I just wasn't expecting to see her. At my house, where she'd been alone with the walking hormone I called my son. Her car wasn't in the driveway so she would have had to ride home from school with Cole and Emma. Why had neither of my children mentioned this to me? Especially Emma.

Paisley climbed onto one of the barstools at the counter, pretty as ever. "Hey Miss Logan. Can I help you with supper?" And as sweet as ever.

I couldn't let the rules bend so easily, no matter how sweet. "Um...maybe. Ah, Cole, when we talked on the phone earlier, did you forget to mention Paisley was coming home with you? You know the rules."

Paisley jerked to attention. "Oh no! Miss Logan, I'm sorry. It's my fault. I was scared to drive in the snow and asked him for a ride."

"She drove into a ditch last time the weather was bad and now she's a little spooked," Cole said like that made everything okay.

It didn't, but I could understand her fear. I had driven

white-knuckled many times through snow and sleet. Still, I didn't like them alone in the house. I didn't like not knowing she was here, and I certainly didn't like that she would probably have to spend the night. Cole and I *would* have a discussion about this later.

I took an onion from the wire bucket on the counter and slapped it and the cutting board in front of Paisley. I handed her the knife with a smile. "Start cutting."

Cole took the barstool beside her. "What are we having?"

I tossed him a couple potatoes and the peeler. "Goulash."

Paisley lifted her sculpted brows. "What's *goulash*?"

Cole jumped right in. "It's a Hungarian soup. Perfect for days like today."

Impressed, but suspicious the kid sitting in front of me wasn't *my* son, I asked, "Where'd you learn that?"

"Doretha. Isn't that where you learned to make it?"

Goulash, cornbread, and cherry crunch cake. Not to mention some damn good biscuits. "She taught me everything I know how to do in the kitchen." Everything I knew how to do in *life*.

After browning the ground beef, I tossed it, the potatoes, onions, elbow macaroni and a can of crushed tomatoes into a soup pot and let it simmer. When Cole and Paisley started back upstairs, I steered them toward the sunroom by sharply clearing my throat. Not long after, Ivy squealed a symphony of giggles accompanied by Cole saying he was going to get her. Amazing how he paid so much attention to the toddler in the presence of his girlfriend.

I called Paisley's parents to assure them their daughter was safe. I also volunteered Grayson to take her home sometime the next day. Although the weather played a part in the girl having to spend the night at our house, some devious thought went into the planning. I was sure of that.

I fixed myself a cup of hot tea and watched it snow. We'd end up with more than a foot if it fell like this overnight. How deep would it have to get before Grayson would postpone the recovery? My interest in Dr. Felicia Scranton and the crime scene wavered between obsessed and non-existent. There was no in between. Risk frost bite versus finding more human remains. Whoever they belonged to, whether it was Kelvin or Katherine, the discovery of a human skull with a slug in it was a story.

We ate supper at seven in the dining room. Paisley complimented the soup and Cole responded by taking credit for peeling the potatoes. Ivy balked at the idea of soup and instead munched happily on chicken nuggets. Around seven thirty, headlights crept up the driveway. The blue glow from the halogen lights brushed the ice-covered windows, turning the glass into a crystal mosaic. Finn stirred at my feet then hopped up and trotted to the backdoor in the kitchen. Grayson was such a fixture around the house these days, Finn no longer barked when Grayson came in.

I he him at the door and greeted him with a soft kiss. As he removed his coat, hat, and gloves, I carried them to the laundry room and hung them over the washer to drip dry. He was down to wool socks, thermal-lined jeans and his Jackson Creek Sheriff's Department sweatshirt when I rejoined him.

"Hungry?" I asked

He pulled me to him, nibbling on my neck. His hands, chilled but not cold, ran up my sides underneath my sweater. "For you."

"Mmm." Remembering we weren't alone, I pulled away.

"We have company. Paisley's here."

"Paisley? I didn't see her car." He looked out the window like he had missed something.

I placed my finger on my lips to hint we should whisper. "Yeah. She didn't drive. Cole brought her here from school."

He struggled to contain a smart-ass grin. "Purposely snowed in. Kind of clever."

I answered with a frown. "Don't be smug. I'm not happy about it."

After dinner, with Paisley safely tucked into Emma's bed alongside my daughter, I poked my head into Cole's room. He was sitting in bed with his phone in his hands, leaning against the headboard. The screen glowed blue in the otherwise dark room.

"Phone off, Cole. It's bedtime."

His thumbs moved across the screen. "Okay. I'm just telling Paisley goodnight."

The phone dinged with an incoming text. With slight stubble dotting his chin, a baritone voice in place of the higher pitched squeak, and towering over me by at least five inches, he was growing into a man. Yet, the grinning child with the wide eyes in front of me was still so much a little boy.

"Goodnight, Cole."

"Night, Mom."

I started out then stopped and turned back. Quietly, I said, "I don't think I need to remind you about the rules for tomorrow if Paisley's still here. Right?"

He put his phone on his nightstand then slid down under the black and teal comforter emblazed with the Carolina

Panthers logo. Santa Claus brought it to him several years ago. "We're cool, Mom."

I stood there for a moment and watched my son settle in for the night. I didn't trust him as far as I could see him. But I did trust that Emma would rat him out.

At the other end of the hallway, Grayson was in my room stripping down to his boxer briefs. With the drapes open and the outside world visible through the exposed windows, the backyard flood lights illuminated the falling snow. My body ached to be with him from the romantic atmosphere alone. I pushed aside the feeling of hypocrisy aimed at the teenagers down the hall and closed the bedroom door.

CHAPTER 4

The next day, after laying down the ground rules with the kids, I dressed as warmly as possible and met Grayson and Dr. Felicia Scranton where the little beagle had found the bones. Two deputies and a crime scene tech joined us.

Grayson introduced Dr. Scranton and we shook hands. About my age, she held it well with a dewy, porcelain complexion that complemented flaming red hair. Round-framed glasses highlighted eager eyes. She wore fuchsia-colored snow bibs and matching boots.

"Okay," she said, clasping her hands together. "Let's get started before it gets any colder."

She directed the techs and Grayson like chess pieces on a snow-covered board. I sat on a boulder to watch.

Dr. Scranton tightened her ponytail, readying for action. "You said you have the skull, right?"

"The skull and a couple smaller bones," Grayson said.

"May I see the pictures?"

The tech with the camera stepped over to her, scrolling through the photos he'd collected so far.

After staring into the viewfinder, nose scrunched, she said,

"Appears to be Caucasian."

The tech studied the photo. "How can you tell?"

Dr. Scranton pointed to the image. "The nasal cavity and jaw. See how narrow the nose area is?"

By the time we broke for lunch, they had uncovered the pelvic bone, a femur, and a couple ribs. The pelvic bone confirmed the bones belonged to a male. I crossed Kimberly Douglas off the list.

After securing the scene, Dr. Scranton rode with Grayson to Minnie's Cafe while I followed. It would have to be a quick lunch for me—I was under a serious deadline. I had to get the pictures and article uploaded if the story was going to make this edition.

The roads weren't great but passable for an experienced driver. Apparently, others in Jackson Creek felt the roads safe enough to venture out. The cafe parking lot was jammed with 4-Wheel drives. Minnie's grandson had scraped the gravel lot with his tractor and pushed the foot of snow into high piles along the edge. Dirt, mud and debris marred the once pristine white fluff, making the mounds look like discarded hope—tarnished, ugly and full of stuff that didn't belong.

Inside, we stamped our boots at the door. The diner was noisy with chatter, clanging dishes, and orders being yelled to the kitchen. The smell of strong coffee and homemade pie competed with the odor of hot peanut oil that seemed to seep from the walls. You didn't have to look at a calendar to know the day of the week around Minnie's. Wednesdays were liver and onions, Friday was hotdogs and fries. You could smell it from the outside. Today was Tuesday, so we were safe with meatloaf.

Diane, part owner and head waitress, called out to us on her way to the kitchen. "There's a booth in the back. Be with you in a minute."

We made our way through the maze of tables and people stopping us for a chat. Most wanted to know from me if the paper was going to be on schedule and if I could give a clue about the headline. I'd laugh and say they'd have to wait and read it.

Grayson ushered Dr. Scranton into one side of the booth then slid in beside her. I sat across from them.

Diane dropped three menus and sets of silverware wrapped in paper napkins on the table. "What can I get y'all to drink?"

Grayson and I both ordered iced tea while Dr. Scranton scrunched her nose, again. "Do you have hot tea?"

Diane shook her head while a grin toyed with her lips. "Not here, sweetie. I can get you some coffee or some hot chocolate if you're wanting something hot."

Dr. Scranton sighed. "I'll just take water, with a slice of lemon, please."

Diane nodded then headed off to fill the drink order.

I toyed with the paper napkin wondering if continuing the profile piece over lunch was acceptable. Whether or not it was, I dove in. "So where are you from, Dr. Scranton?"

"Please, call me Felicia. And Chicago. Born and raised."

"How'd you end up at Appalachia State?" Grayson asked.

"Believe it or not, coming from a city like Chicago, I really enjoy the relaxed surroundings. The quiet is good for the soul."

Diane returned with our drinks then yelled back into the kitchen that table five was still waiting on their pecan pie. She turned back to us and smiled. "Ready to order?"

I grinned at the *quiet*. "Turkey club."

Grayson ordered a burger while Felicia went back and forth between the chicken salad and the southwestern salad. "Does the southwestern salad have black beans, or is it tofu?"

Diane never raised a brow, didn't snicker. Just spouted the facts. "Honey, you ain't gonna find tofu anything in these parts."

"Okay, I'll have the chicken salad. And can you do that with low-fat mayo?"

"Sure can." Diane carried her lie and our orders back to the kitchen.

Grayson and I smiled at one another, knowing full well there wasn't anything low-fat served in Minnie's Café.

Felicia stared at her glass of water as if she just realized there was no lemon slice floating around in it. Rather than bring it to Diane's attention, she moved on. "Tell me about your little paper."

My chest tightened as if the air had been squeezed out of it. *Little paper?* "Um...well, the *Jackson Creek Chronicle* has been in business fourteen years and we have a nice circulation for an ad-supported *little* paper."

A flush spread across her cheeks. "I'm sorry. I didn't mean to offend you."

I waved her off. "It's okay. Sometimes even I'm surprised that we've been in business as long as we have."

"Ava started the paper herself." The pride in Grayson's voice made me smile.

"Really? What made you decide to start a newspaper?"

I fiddled with my napkin, watching the miniscule white fibers roll between my fingers. The answer brought back memories, both good and bad. "There weren't many jobs available in the area for a young mother, so I created one."

That was part of the truth. The other part I remembered was being devastated reading the accounts of my family's sordid past in the large daily paper distributed a hundred miles away, screaming at the words on the newsprint that they were wrong.

In the rush to get the story out there, no one bothered to check that it was right.

Felicia studied me for a moment. "You have children?"

"Three."

"What does your husband do?"

The sting of the question burnt out years ago. Now, the answer was a simple matter of fact. "He's dead."

I despised the sympathetic look that usually followed. It felt hypocritical to even acknowledge it. Cold as it seemed, Tommy's death simply meant I didn't get the chance to tell him to go to hell.

"I'm sorry. Was it an accident?"

"He was killed in the line of duty."

"He was a cop?"

"A deputy with the Jackson County Sheriff's department."

Felicia turned and looked at Grayson. "Was that before your time?"

"Before I was sheriff, yes."

I hurried to put an end to that conversation. "So, basically...I started the paper because I was a lousy stay-at-home mom and there just weren't many opportunities around. And it grew to what it is now."

Diane couldn't have picked a better moment than right then to bring our food. I wasn't sure what it was about Felicia Scranton that rubbed me the wrong way. "Burger for the sheriff, turkey club for Ava and chicken salad for y'all's friend. Get you anything else?"

Felicia gushed over the size of her plate of chicken salad and laughingly asked for a box to go. "Since we're going to be outside, I guess I don't need to worry about keeping it refrigerated."

After taking a bite of my sandwich, I circled back to the purpose of Felicia's visit. "How long will it take before we get any tests results back on the remains?"

"Anywhere from a couple days to several weeks. Unfortunately, it's a cold case and they seldom take priority." She looked at Grayson for confirmation.

"Ava's already started going through the yearbook from the class of '67. We'll compare it with missing persons. Process of elimination."

Felicia looked skeptical, and if I had to guess, my involvement with the case puzzled her. "You two always work together on cases like this?" She wagged a finger between us.

"Not always," Grayson said. Maybe a little too quickly.

"I've learned through the years what needs to be withheld. I've never burned him."

Felicia held my gaze until it bordered on awkward. "It's just a little unusual, that's all. Probably one of the perks of being a small paper."

She dug into her chicken salad, happily devouring full-fat mayo without knowing it. "So, back to the bones. How long do you anticipate before you can clear the scene?"

"Oh, we'll clear it in a day or so, but we'll continue the excavation for several weeks."

Several weeks? "Do you have the manpower for that?" I asked Grayson.

Before he could answer, Felicia shook her head. "I'll use students. Cheaper on everyone."

I understood the thought behind using students, but could their findings stand up in court? "Are these third- or fourth-year students?"

Felicia speared a fork-full of salad. "Don't worry, I'll oversee everything. Students are usually excited about it, you know? They're there because they want to be, not because they're getting paid. What have you found so far in the yearbook?"

I told her about the four boys. "Kelvin Dennis deserves another look. The only other one could be Kenneth Dupree. The only records I could find by that name, though, are for a guy from Knoxville."

"He could have moved," Grayson said.

That was true. "I'll dig a little deeper on him."

Felicia grinned, waving her fork at Grayson. "Your department does have detectives, doesn't it?"

Grayson inhaled then released the breath slowly. "He's on vacation this week."

"I'm the next best thing." I finished off my turkey club, savoring every single mayo-smothered bite.

CHAPTER 5

I went by the office after lunch while Grayson and Felicia headed back to the scene. Despite the snow and a fresh crime scene, I had a paper to get out. The bones would still be bones tomorrow. Danny's F-150 was in the office parking lot. The only tire tracks in the snow were from his truck. The gravel lot didn't have marked spaces, but even if it did, they'd be buried beneath the snow. I parked beside Danny, leaving plenty of room for spinning tires.

Inside, he was at his desk glaring at both monitors filled with the latest issue of the *Jackson Creek Chronicle*. He glanced at me then turned back to his work.

Danny Olson had been my layout man since the first issue when I had a big idea and little knowledge. I knew how to craft an article from the limited production of a high school newspaper, but had no idea how to pull it all together and produce an actual paper through a web press. He'd worked for the big papers—the *Post*, the *Constitution*—and yet, ended up at the *Jackson Creek Chronicle*, by choice. He said he preferred the slower pace, the feature stories of good-hearted neighbors, and the fewer number of murders splashed across the front page.

I shook out of my coat and hung it on the coat tree. "How's it looking?"

"Better than I thought. If you want to add to the skeleton story, I've got room on page four to continue it. Maybe even add a picture."

I did have enough info to add a couple more paragraphs. "How much do you want?"

"Six, seven 'graphs. Four if you're adding a picture."

This story would probably drag out over a few editions. I'd save the profile piece on Dr. Scranton for later. At my desk, I powered up the computer and built an article around the information we had, which wasn't much but newsworthy just the same. Male, Caucasian. Where, when. Add a quote from Pudge Collins, Sheriff Ridge, Dr. Scranton. Purposely omitted: the bullet wound and the class ring. Facts only the killer would know.

I had just uploaded the article when the bell over the front door jangled and Kristy Beckly burst in, jerking my attention away from my computer. Red faced and gasping for air, she spit words out between breaths. "Ava, come quick. There's been an accident."

Danny and I both leapt up, bumping into one another on our way out the door. Kristy's beat up old truck had slid to a stop, nearly missing my Tahoe.

Aaron Bell, the documentary film maker, was in the passenger side of the cab. In obvious pain, he tried to wave me off when I tore open the door. An old rag of some sort was wrapped around his right hand. There didn't appear to be any blood.

"What happened?"

Kristy nudged herself between me and the truck door. "My

truck was running hot and he stopped to help me. He was gonna add some water, but the radiator cap blew off on him. He got his hand burnt real bad."

Aaron grimaced. "I'm sure it'll be fine," he said, his words clipped and breathless.

"I thought Mary McCarter might could help him, but I don't know where she lives 'xactly."

"I'll take him. Can you get in the Tahoe or do you need help?"

He eased himself out of the truck, cradling his right arm with his left. "If you could just drop me off at Urgent Care, I'll probably be fine."

I ignored him and helped him into my SUV then turned to Danny. "I just uploaded the revision and a couple pictures. I have my cell so call if you have questions."

A minute later, I pulled away and headed deep into the mountains. Mary McCarter lived twenty minutes outside of town at the end of a switchback that emptied into a holler.

The further we moved away from town, the more Aaron's brows creased. "Don't y'all have an Urgent Care?"

I threw him a glance then returned my eyes to the curvy, snow-covered road. "We did. It closed."

He chewed on that a moment, clearly not understanding by the look on his face. "Why would an Urgent Care close?"

"Lost their license for over prescribing opioids."

Aaron didn't say anything but continued to watch me as if gaging the truth in my statement. The silence creeped me out. I said, "See—that's why I don't want anything to do with a documentary. You're judging."

"No, I'm not. This area's not the only area to have an opioid problem, you know? Your mountains don't own the rights to it."

"But you don't hear about it anywhere else like you do 'round here."

A low moan rolled up through his throat and he pulled his injured hand protectively closer to his chest. "Who is this Mary McCarter?"

"A granny witch."

"Great. Just freaking great."

"You wanted true Appalachia."

CHAPTER 6

Mary McCarter lived with her simple-minded son, Keeper, in the family home on a couple acres. The clapboard house with the tin roof sat at the highest point in the bottom of the holler. High enough to deter flooding when the river rose with rain. Mary and Keeper farmed a half acre of the land they owned and often sold or bartered the goods they didn't can and freeze for later. Mary's brother, Roy, moved back to the family land after his wife took off to Florida when he took to the bottle. Now, he lived on the back acre in a trailer and helped with the farming when the mood struck him.

Now in her late sixties, Mary had had Keeper when she was a teenager in a time it wasn't acceptable. An unmarried seventeen-year-old who wouldn't name the father of her baby was shunned. Until someone needed her services. Mary had the *gift*. Everyone in the region knew it; some feared it, but most of us embraced it.

As soon as I pulled into the driveway, Keeper came out on the porch. Tall and lanky with hooded eyes and a head of unruly dark hair, he waved excitedly. Pushing fifty with the mind of an eight-year-old, he got his name when his kinfolk pressured his teenage mother to give the baby away. *He ain't right, ain't right in the head* is what they said. Mary told them her son was just fine. He was a *keeper*.

Aaron stared hard at the house and the man on the porch waving like a child. "Are you going to tell me what a *granny witch* is?"

I helped him unbuckle then opened the door. "Mary can talk the fire out of your hand."

Aaron stared at his hand then at me, a hint of skepticism showing in his eyes.

Keeper came down the steps to greet us, his soft face unusually hard with worry. "Is your friend hurt, Ava?"

"He burnt his hand."

Keeper spun around and hurried back up the steps. "Momma! Come quick."

Aaron and I followed Keeper up onto the porch and through the front door. Aaron giggled under his breath. "I don't think it's *that* much of an emergency."

"Everything's an emergency with Keeper," I whispered.

We stood in the tiny living room, smothering from the warmth of the oil heater. A strong scent of eucalyptus hovered in the air like a low-hanging cloud. One you could touch and walk through. Mary came into the living room, drying her hands on a thread-bare dish towel.

She approached Aaron, took a quick glance at his wrapped hand then motioned for us to follow. "Come on in here."

"Momma'll fix you right up."

Mary McCarter epitomized the back-to-nature, leftover hippie look. Silver hair fell to the middle of her back, corralled into a braided ponytail with a clip. Faded jeans, frayed at the flared bottom, and a well-worn Beatles t-shirt underneath an unbuttoned flannel shirt. She moved her tall and slender frame with the grace of a cat.

In the kitchen, I introduced everyone before taking a seat at the Formica-topped table. Mason jars filled with sprouting herbs sat clustered at one end of the table and throughout the cluttered kitchen wherever there was space on the counter tops. Drying roots hung in bundles from a pots and pans rack suspended from the ceiling. Something was boiling on the decades-old stove and the steam cast a slick sheen on the knotty pine cabinets.

Mary pulled a chair up beside Aaron and gently unwrapped his injured hand. He watched her with a wary eye. We'd know soon enough how *non-judgmental* he truly was.

"Steam burn?" she asked.

Aaron nodded. "Radiator cap."

Mary lightly touched one area of the blistered skin with the tip of her finger. "Those caps can leave some nasty burns."

She closed her eyes for a moment then made the sign of the cross from her forehead to her chest, then across. "Where you from?"

"Washington D.C."

Aaron watched every move she made, which wasn't many. She would blow on the burn then lightly touch the skin. She repeated this process several times.

"What are you doing in this neck of the woods?"

He looked at me as if asking permission to divulge his mission. I saved him the trouble. "Aaron's a documentary filmmaker. He's hoping to make a documentary on Appalachia culture."

Mary lifted her eyes to mine then turned to Aaron. "A movie maker, huh."

"We gonna be in the movies?" Keeper's voice rose with excitement.

Aaron watched Mary tend to his hand with wonder. Judging by the relaxed expression on his face, the pain was subsiding. "It's stuff like this that I want to show. Not the poverty and the drugs."

"Poverty *is* part of the region. It runs as deep as some of the bloodlines," Mary said.

"But it's not all there is. *That's* what I want to show. This right here. People helping people using whatever means they can. You're a...what did you call it, Ava?"

I mumbled, "A granny witch."

"Or, granny *woman*." Mary smiled. Her eyes softened like warmed butter. The corners of her mouth arched upward in the slightest of smiles. She usually shied away from talk about her gifts but she seemed almost eager with Aaron. "You've never heard the term before?"

Aaron was slow to respond, obviously giving his answer some thought. After a long minute, he finally said, "No, not before today. But given what I've seen, I imagine it's just a title that changes from culture to culture."

"You're right. Native Americans, depending on the tribe, have various names. What I practice came from Ireland and Scotland and I blended it with a little Tsalagi tradition"

"Tsalagi?" Aaron asked.

"They're called Cherokee these days."

"What all do you do?"

Mary exhaled then wrinkled her nose and rubbed her fingers over Aaron's palm. The redness had faded to a light pinkish hue, the skin no longer puckered. "Those blisters should fade by tomorrow. Keeper, go get me a roll of cheesecloth, please."

Keeper hopped up then disappeared into a storage pantry beside the backdoor. After rumbling around, he came back with the fabric. "This it, Momma?"

"That's it. Will you get me the scissors?" She rolled out a swath of the cloth then cut it down to bandage size while Keeper looked on like an operating room assistant. Mary wrapped Aaron's hand and wrist then lightly tied off the ends. "Keep it covered tonight. You can take the wrap off in the morning. Don't put any kind of ointment on the wound, and if it's still burning tomorrow, get Ava to bring you back."

Aaron nodded. His gaze wandered around the cluttered kitchen, taking in the sprouting roots and drying herbs. "Are these the tools of the trade?"

"Some of them. I keep my black cauldron out back."

His eyes widened before narrowing into a suspicious squint. "You're joking?"

Mary grinned as she threw me a glance. The misconception about women with the gift, whether they were called granny witches, granny women, or medicine women, seemed only to exist with outsiders. The locals understood.

I answered for her. "Yes, she's just kidding. It's actually in the shed beside her broom."

Everyone got a good laugh, even Keeper. Mary secured the roll of cheesecloth then handed it to her son to put away. He hopped up, still giggling

"What does a granny witch, or *woman*, do, exactly?"

Mary got up and busied herself around the kitchen. "Ava can tell you later. How's the hand feeling?"

Aaron stared at his hand as if he had forgotten it was there. Maybe he had. "It doesn't burn anymore."

"Good. So is this your first film?" She poured boiling water into four mismatched coffee mugs then added heaping spoonfuls of spiced tea.

"No. I've got three to my credit. My best one is *Easter's Promise*. It's about a non-profit horse farm helping veterans with PTSD. Especially Vietnam veterans."

Mary snickered and looked over her shoulder at Aaron. "What do you know about Vietnam? That was way before your time."

"My father did two tours. He's not disabled but he has buddies who are. It's a subject pretty close to heart."

My mind went back to the yearbook from the class of '67 and the ones who never came home from the war. Keith Jessup Davis and Kenneth James Dupree.

Mary started over to the table with the mugs. I jumped up to help her and took one, setting it on the table. When I reached for the other, my fingers slid across hers causing Mary to recoil in shock. My breath hitched as I too felt the jolt. I jerked my hand back, barely avoiding the slosh of the scalding liquid.

"What the—" I squealed. That wasn't a static electricity zap associated with winter dryness. That was something much more. And Mary knew it, too.

She hurried to put down the mugs then whirled around to face me. "He has dark hair."

I couldn't speak as my mind ricocheted in a thousand directions. Who has dark hair? Her face pulled into a tight knot of confusion. I'd witnessed Mary's moments of insight before but not like this. I'd never seen her this rattled.

"Mary, what do you see?"

Her knees buckled and she grabbed the counter for support. I lunged to steady her before she hit the ground.

"Momma!" Keeper leapt up and rushed to his mother. Together, we walked her back to the table and eased her into a chair.

Color drained from her face, leaving a ghastly white pallor in its place. Frantic, Keeper shook her bony shoulders. "Momma. What's wrong? Are you dying?"

I moved him to the side and pulled his hands away from his mother. "Keeper—she's going to be okay. Give her some air." I swallowed my own fear while working to calm him.

"I...I...I don't want my momma to die."

"She's not going to die, Keeper. I won't let her."

Mary clasped her trembling hands and held them in her lap. Her breathing verged on hyperventilation as she stared at something only she could see. I wanted so bad to see it, too.

"Can I do anything?" Aaron asked, his voice filled with concern.

I answered with a shake of my head then knelt in front of Mary. "What do you see?"

"Death. I see death. All around you."

Chapter 7

I backed away from Mary, my hands shaking. Air hung in my lungs. She had to be referring to the remains. At least I hoped she was. I believed in everything Mary practiced, including her gift of insight, but this time her vision spooked me.

"Whose death?" I said.

Color slowly crept back into her cheeks. Her breathing settled back into normal rhythm. Keeper handed her the mug she had almost dropped earlier.

She took a tiny sip. "I don't know whose death. I just know...they had dark hair. And I see...I see it around you, Ava. An aura, maybe? I just don't know."

I had never seen Mary McCarter rattled. Confused. Frightened. She wasn't herself. "Pudge Collins and I found human remains near the old mill yesterday. It looks like they've been there awhile. Could that be the aura you're seeing?"

No one spoke for a minute as they processed the information. Finally, Keeper whispered to his mother, "What does that mean, Momma?"

"It means they found a skeleton."

His eyes grew huge as shock registered on his face. "Like a

spooky skeleton?"

Mary fixed her eyes on mine. Still uncertain. She was leaving it to me to explain the discovery to her son.

"Yeah. Like a spooky skeleton," I mumbled.

"Ain't that sump'ng, Momma? Ava found a real live skeleton. Can I go see it?"

"No, Son. I imagine the sheriff's department is looking into it now." She cut her eyes back up to mine. "Any idea who it belongs to?"

"We have no way of knowing until they can run some tests."

Aaron joined the conversation. "Does Jackson Creek have the equipment to run those kinds of tests?"

If he'd researched the area before showing up at my office, he'd know that answer. "A doctor of anthropology from the university is helping out," I said.

Mary finished her tea then stood and wobbled. Either frayed nerves or old knees. I offered a hand to steady her. She stared at my gesture with the same apprehension of someone facing off with a growling dog.

"Do you still see the aura?" I asked.

She took her time answering then took my hand with an obvious amount of caution. "It's not as strong."

When the skin-to-skin contact didn't produce any electrical charge, Mary moved with more confidence. She gathered up the mugs from the table whether we were finished with the tea or not and dropped them into the porcelain sink. "How's the hand?" she said to Aaron.

"Good."

"Don't put salve or anything on it." She pulled a cluster of herbs from a hanging wire basket and spread them on a well-used cutting board.

She was still rattled. She'd already given him those instructions. I looked at Aaron then tilted my head toward the door. Mary's hint that it was time for the company to leave wasn't hard to miss.

On the way back to town, Aaron continued staring at his hand, clearly wanting to remove the bandage to get a better look at Mary's powers. "I should have paid her *something.*"

"You don't pay for services. Only for products."

"And the products would be...?"

"Tonics. Salves. That kind of stuff."

The closer we got to town, the less snow covered the road. But mounds of it stood like miniature ice-capped mountains along the shoulders. The kids would go to school tomorrow. Regardless, Paisley wasn't spending the night again.

"Where did you stop to help Kristy?"

"It was a—" he hesitated, chewing his words as much as his bottom lip. "A...ah, rehab center. It's a two-story brick building."

I knew exactly where it was. Everyone in Jackson Creek knew where it was. A quarter of the population had been through its doors as more than visitors. The majority of patients used to have a problem with the bottle. Now their demons existed in prescription pill bottles.

Despite wanting to bore a hole straight through him with a sideways glance, I kept my eyes on the road. He wanted to show *the good side of Appalachia*, my sweet ass. And given his hesitation in divulging where he'd helped Kristy, he wasn't comfortable with me knowing. "What were you doing at the rehab center?"

"I wasn't there. Kristy was."

That made no sense. Certainly someone at a medical facility would be capable of tending to a burn. "Why didn't she just take you inside the center?"

Aaron watched the piles of snow roll by like they were really interesting. "She has a complicated life." His concern seemed genuine.

A laugh bubbled up and trickled from the corner of my mouth. "Let me guess...she was checking up on her on-again-off-again boyfriend, Rudy Meyers, to see if he was there but didn't want him to know."

Aaron smiled. "See—that's exactly why you should be the one to help me with this documentary. You *do* know these people."

Kristy couldn't take Aaron inside because if Rudy was there, he'd see her. "And she couldn't leave her truck there because then he'd know what she was up to, so she hurried you up to add some water to the radiator. How am I doing so far?"

"Oh, I'd say pretty good."

Right after we passed the rehab center, I eased off the road behind a parked Land Rover. "That yours?"

"Yeah. Kind of nice seeing it still has all its wheels. If it was parked like that in D.C., it'd be stripped to the frame."

"We're not fast enough to steal the wheels, but I'd check the stereo system."

He had an easy laugh and no matter how much I wanted to dislike him, there really wasn't a reason to. "I would like to know more about granny witches," he said.

I slowly shook my head. "That falls right into the idea of the *mountain people* cliché."

"It depends on how it's presented."

I didn't have an answer or a comeback. It was a true statement.

"Just take a look at one of my films. You'll change your

mind."

I didn't want to change my mind. I didn't want anything to do with Aaron Bell or his films. "I can introduce you to a historian over at the university. He can help you a lot more than me."

The thought lingered for a nano-second "I don't want history. I want the 'now.' The present. I don't care about the legends and tall-tales."

I jerked my head around and glared at him. "What do you think a granny witch is?"

He jerked the bandage off then waved his hand in my direction. "What do you think this is?"

Anger notched my voice up and I shot back, "A fact. That's what it is."

"Exactly."

Startled he agreed with me, it took a second for the realization to cultivate.

"With your help, I can show this—" He jabbed his arm out further for emphasis. "For what it truly is. Not a cliché. Not some kind of tall-tale. But a way of life."

I wasn't going to argue for its own sake. And because he was right. Mary's and all the other granny women before her and those present shared a way of being, a centuries-old tradition that was still practiced today. Like the blue-tipped mountains surrounding us, their gifts were part of the landscape of Appalachia's very existence.

It *was* a way of life. Reluctantly, I said, "Let me watch one of your films tonight. I'll call you sometime tomorrow."

"Watch the one on Vietnam. Mary would probably even like that one."

CHAPTER 8

A few cop cars, including Grayson's Expedition, remained at the edge of the field near the crime scene. I pulled beside them but didn't kill the engine. Not yet. Pushing four o'clock, the temperature hovered around the freezing mark. The sky dark and foreboding.

Had Grayson been here all day? Had Dr. Scranton? I finally shut off the Tahoe and braced myself for the cold.

I ducked under the yellow tape bordering the scene. The tent had been moved about ten yards from the original site. Beneath the weather-proof protection, Grayson and Dr. Scranton knelt beside a tarp covered with bones fashioned into a crude half-there skeleton.

Grayson looked up as I approached and gave me a wink. "Hey. How's the paper coming along?"

"We'll make deadline. Thanks to Danny, of course."

Dr. Scranton stared at me then crinkled her nose, causing her glasses to rise up the bridge. "Are you publishing anything about our John Doe?"

"Lead story."

She turned to Grayson. "Is that wise?"

Excuse me? I was standing right there. My eye twitched at the doctor's rudeness.

After a silent moment too long for my comfort, Grayson answered. "It won't hurt anything. It might even help."

Might?

Dr. Scranton eased back on her haunches and used her forearm to brush stray wisps of ginger hair from her face. "If you say so. I've just never seen a reporter with this much access to a crime scene."

Despite the freezing temperature, heat bubbled up in my chest and scorched my insides. I was standing right in front of her, damnitt. In front of *them*. I felt like a chastised child waiting on a scolding from Mommy and Daddy. I'd be damned if they were going to tell me what I could and couldn't publish.

She leaned into Grayson, almost whispering. "It's your crime scene. As long as you're comfortable with it, I guess I don't really have a say-so."

Grayson glanced at me, cheeks flushing with the tiniest hint of red. "It's fine."

I spoke carefully so I didn't spit the words. "Maybe you should read a few past issues to familiarize yourself with the paper. They're archived online."

Her mouth twitched. "I didn't mean to offend you."

That was the second time today she'd said that. For someone who *didn't mean to*, she was racking up the points. It was childish, I knew it was, but my female intuition was on high alert. The way she leaned into Grayson, the whisper. "What time will you be home? Should I wait up?" I said directly to him. No mistake there. No lines to read between.

He blinked those pale blue eyes several times, unsure how to respond. I almost felt guilty for putting him on the spot like that. Our relationship was public knowledge but we didn't advertise it. "Um...yeah. It won't be as late as last night."

"Great. So how *is* John Doe coming along?" I bent over, hands on my knees, and stared at the skeleton like I knew what I was looking at. I'd fake it before I'd let her know I might as well have been trying to read Greek.

Grayson handed me his notepad. "White male, approximately eighteen to twenty-five years old. Average height."

I had all that but the age range. Still, I deciphered his scribblings and jotted them down in my own notebook, anyway. "What is average height? Six feet?"

Dr. Scranton looked from me to Grayson, back to me, back to Grayson. Her eyes narrowed. It wasn't a difficult question but her suspicion flickered like a waning light bulb. Finally, she answered, "Five foot ten to six feet. More or less."

More or less? "Any idea of build?"

She arranged two bones where the leg would go. "Can't tell that from the bones unless the person was morbidly obese."

I stared at the skull. The hole where the shot entered was smaller than a dime—though the damage had been done inside, the bullet pinballing through the soft tissue of the brain.

"And so far," Dr. Scranton continued, "from what I can tell the damage to the skeleton was natural deterioration."

No dismemberment. Thank God. Some things just didn't happen in Jackson Creek. Still, there was a skull with a bullet in it and bones that had been buried. Someone died a violent death in Jackson Creek. It wasn't unheard of. The town'd had its share of violence. More recently, the quest for oxy and Vicodin led people to do stupid things. Before that, it was moonshine and property lines.

No matter how much it irked me to leave the scene, giving Dr. Scranton a one-up, I was freezing my ass off. I was anxious to get back to the yearbook and laptop. I told Grayson I'd see him at home, on purpose, then trudged back to the Tahoe. Dusk was fast approaching and shrouded the field with a dingy gray backdrop. I loathed winter.

I called Doretha from the car to get her brother Calvin's phone number. Maybe he would remember something from his time at the mill. Or remember if someone with the initials KJD worked there.

After coming up with a plan in case of no school tomorrow, we hung up and I called Calvin. When Emma was a newborn, Calvin and his wife brought a baby gift and a chicken casserole out to the house. Last time I saw him was at Tommy's funeral.

He answered on the second ring and I recognized his voice right off. "Calvin, it's Ava Logan."

"Ava Logan. My, my. How are you, child?"

"I'm good. I hope y'all are."

"Bertie's got the arthritis in her knees but still hobbling around."

We exchanged small talk for a few minutes, catching up on life's ups and downs. "Hey Calvin, I'm working on a story that involves the old mill. I was wondering if I could stop by and talk to you about it."

"You don't say. I reckon that'd be all right."

"Do you mind if I come now?" Their mill house wasn't far from the crime scene.

"That'll be fine. You know where we are."

I pulled away heading to Calvin and Miss Bertie's, then called home. Emma answered. "Everything okay?" I said.

"Yeah. Paisley's mom came and got her after lunch. She

said the roads would probably ice back over after dark."

True. Maybe Paisley's parents shared my concern about more than just the roads.

"Think we'll have school tomorrow?" Emma said.

"Probably get delayed. Look, I've got one more interview to do then I'll be on home."

"What are we having for supper?"

The dreaded question. I'd been so slack lately, averaging one or two cooked meals a week. "I...don't know."

"Can we have breakfast?"

"You mean like bacon and eggs and homemade biscuits?" It did sound tempting but the biscuits would have to come from a can tonight. I wasn't up to being covered in flour.

"Um...no. Breakfast like cereal."

It didn't take much for me to agree. I clicked the phone off and tossed it in my bag.

Calvin and Bertie Andrews lived in the same tiny house they'd lived in all their married life. They'd raised three kids there. When the mill closed, the renters had first option to buy the homes formerly owned by the corporation. Calvin and Bertie jumped at the opportunity.

Their thousand-square foot home sat among twenty others just like it in a neighborhood simply called the mill village. Most of the residents were good people. Others weren't but that often came with the territory.

I parked on the street in front of the white, vinyl-sided house with black shutters. A small front stoop with wrought iron handrails framed the front like welcoming arms. Calvin met me at the door and wrapped me in a tight hug. God had given Calvin and Doretha arms made just for hugging. He was a small-framed man with the strength of an ox.

A yapping little dog with cloudy eyes sniffed my ankles until Calvin shooed it away. "Ain't you a sight," he said, stepping back to get a better look. Dressed in soft, faded jeans that bunched at the waist underneath his belt, he hobbled with a bent back to his recliner. "Pretty as ever. Come on in here. Bertie's done gone to the grocery store to get some snacks for the grandkids. They coming to visit tomorrow."

The small living room gave testament to the pride Calvin and Bertie had in their family. Framed pictures and awards, tokens of family vacations. Despite the abundance, the room wasn't cluttered. It was warm and inviting. The smell of supper simmering in the next room added to the comfort.

Calvin waved me over to the sofa then eased into his well-worn chair. A safety net of sorts. The dog hopped into his lap and settled there. "So you're doing an article on the old mill?"

In a round-about way. "I am. Sort of."

"It was a good place to work back then. Hated to see it close."

"Kept food on a lot of people's table 'round here, I suppose."

He slowly nodded, a tiny smile curling his lips. "That it did."

I settled into the sofa, preferring conversation over interviewing. "What years did you work at the mill?"

"Let's see...me and Bertie'd been married about a year. We got married in '65 so I'm guessing around 1966."

"Were you there in 1967?"

"I was there 'til they closed the doors in 1988."

July third, to be exact. Grayson seemed to have the date etched in his memory. "Do you remember anyone with the initials KJD?"

His face crinkled into a tight knot, the skin aged and

leathery. After a long moment, he shook his head. "No, can't say that I do. Course there was right many people worked there back in the day."

"Do you ever remember hearing tale of an argument carrying over outside of work?"

A toothy smile spread across his face. "Boys always be fighting about somethin'. This one here done run off with that one's wife or the dogs got loose and scared the baby. You name it, they'll fight about it."

"Was it ever serious enough to get physical?"

The smile faded as a memory seemed to take hold. Reflective, he said quietly, "Physical or violent?"

I didn't understand what he meant and he obviously saw my confusion.

"Physical would be two or three good ol' boys taking a couple swings at one another. Maybe busting a beer bottle over one another's head. Violent is when them good ol' boys mean to do some harm."

A bullet to the head would fall into the latter. "Violent."

He nodded, exhaling a slow breath, then looked up at me and smiled again. "Lord, child—I ain't even offered you a drink. Would you like some tea or maybe a cup of coffee?"

"I'm fine, Calvin. But thanks just the same. So, do you remember a situation at the mill that might have turned violent?"

He cocked his head and glared at me through squinting eyes. "Whatcho got up your sleeve, girl?"

The tone of the question threw me. A jolt I wouldn't have thought Calvin Andrews capable of giving. "Something happened at the mill a long time ago. I'm just trying to get to the bottom of it."

He nodded again. Rolled his tongue around in his cheeks. Stroked the little dog. "You best write about somethin' that matters. Ain't nothin' ever happened at the mill worth writing about."

Calvin knew more than he was telling.

CHAPTER 9

Was this going to be a game of "I'll tell you what I know if you do the same?" I moved to the edge of the sofa and spoke quietly. "Calvin, skeletal remains were found near the mill yesterday. They're still trying to identify who they belong to."

Calvin turned his eyes away, looking at everything in the room except me. "Wish I could help."

"Did one of those arguments maybe go a little too far?"

He spat a laugh. "I didn't 'xactly hang around with my co-workers when the shift was over. They did their thing and I came home to Bertie. I weren't a carouser."

"Were the other guys?"

"Some were. Most were just good ol' boys trying to make a living."

Which category did KJD fit into? "Did anyone associated with the mill ever go missing?"

"You mean like one of the workers?"

"Yeah. Do you ever remember hearing about an employee that may have disappeared?"

He gave it some thought then shook his head. "Not that I can recollect."

We stared at one another until it became awkward. He turned toward one of the framed pictures on an end table. He and Bertie with their arms wrapped around a West Point graduate. Grandson maybe?

"That's Calvin Lee Andrews III," he said, his voice soft as a feather. "That was a proud, proud day."

There was a bigger picture behind the grandfather's pride, the old mill, and whoever had died in the barren field. If I could only connect the dots.

"Is he the one coming to visit?"

He beamed with pride, the skin around his eyes creasing into tiny lines. "He is. Graduated second in his class. He's a good boy. Or maybe I should say *man*."

We chuckled, and although I needed the information I hoped he could provide, I didn't push him. I enjoyed seeing how proud he was of his grandson. Given all that could go wrong in today's world, it was a nice moment to share.

"He sends me and Bertie a birthday card every year. Ain't missed a year since he was old enough to address the envelope. Bertie's kept ''em all, too. Got 'em tucked away in a drawer back there in the bedroom. She keeps everything, that Bertie." He waved his hand like he was waving off the sentimentality. We both knew better.

I gently steered the talk back to the mill. "Calvin, do you remember if any of the guys at the mill might have had a beef with a co-worker? Or with anyone in town, maybe?"

"Like I told you earlier, those boys were always up to something. Most of the time, they didn't mean no harm."

"Harm came to the remains that were found, Calvin. Someone who worked at the mill at that time might know something."

"You sure I can't get you a glass of tea or coffee?"

I shook my head. Moved to the edge of the sofa. "No, I'm fine. Do you remember the names of any of your co-workers? A Kenneth Dupree or maybe Kelvin Dennis?"

He gave serious thought to it for a moment then asked, "How's Tommy doing?"

Stunned, I stared at Calvin. The question grabbed my heart and squeezed the breath from me. "Tommy's dead, Calvin. He died when Emma was a baby. You came to his funeral."

He slowly nodded. "I hate to hear that."

"You don't remember his funeral? You and Bertie came."

"He's a deputy sheriff." He struggled up from the recliner, wobbled over to me. "I need to check on supper. Bertie's got it on the stove and she'll kill me dead if I burn it up."

He lightly touched my shoulder, perhaps a gentle way to usher me to the door. Laughing, he patted my back as I stood. "Tell Tommy I said hey. You two come have supper with us one night."

I stood at the front door long after he'd closed it wondering what in the hell had just happened. I then drove home running the conversation over again in my head. Calvin *had* avoided the question about trouble at the mill. No imagination there. The whole bit about Tommy...did he honestly not remember? If that was the case, could I trust his memory about the mill? By the time I pulled into our driveway, daylight was history. Amber-colored lights from the house glowed in the distance like lightning bugs trapped in a mason jar. The snow that hadn't melted yet shimmered in the brush of headlights.

Grayson's Expedition sat parked at the end of the drive. My eyes immediately went to the dashboard clock. What was he doing here at six o'clock?

I grabbed my bag and notebook then hurried inside. Finn met me at the door, turning circles until I acknowledged her with a pat. Grayson, Emma, and Ivy were in the kitchen at the table. Ivy wiggled from Grayson's lap and ran to me, arms spread wide with chubby fingers saying *Gimme*. I hoisted her to my hip then smothered her with kisses. Puffy rims surrounded Emma's red-streaked eyes.

My chest tightened as if someone reached in and twisted my heart into knots. "What's the matter?"

"Where were you?" my daughter said, the sudden snap venomous.

I put Ivy down. "Following up on a story. What's going on?"

Grayson shared a tiny smile then tried to explain. "There was a car in the driveway and Emma got a little spooked. She couldn't reach you, so she called me."

"Who was it?"

He shrugged slightly. Ever the peacekeeper. "They were gone by the time I got here."

I turned to Emma, her face flushed with anger. I fought to control the panic rising in my voice. "How long were they here?"

"I don't know. Long enough. He wouldn't get out. He just sat there."

I instinctively glanced at the staircase leading upstairs. My sixteen-year-old son, the protector. "Where was Cole?"

"Facetiming with Paisley." Emma rolled her eyes.

Grayson moved over in the booth to make room for me. I slid in beside him. "Did you get a good look at the driver?" I asked Emma.

"No. The windows were tinted."

"What kind of car was it?"

"I don't know. A big SUV like yours."

Most everyone I knew from these parts drove SUV's or trucks. The weight and four-wheel drive helped with snow and the occasional landslide. "I'm sorry you were scared, honey. I'll take a look at the security camera. It may have just been someone from the power company. They have those new hand-held meter readers where they don't even have to get out of the car."

It was a stretch and I wasn't even sure it was time for the electric bill. But if it would set her mind at ease, I'd lie. Hopefully, the security camera aimed at the driveway would confirm my thoughts.

I went over to the counter to retrieve the source of the problem. Except it wasn't there. Frantic, I dug through my bag, piling everything from my notepad to baby wipes to a bottle of ibuprofen and a pack of fruit snacks on the counter. No phone.

I scrambled outside to the Tahoe and found my phone in the passenger side floorboard. Six missed calls, all from Emma. Crestfallen, I went back inside.

"Why didn't you answer it?" She had a valid concern, especially since she was babysitting a toddler.

"It must have fallen out of my bag. I'm so sorry, Emma."

The apology landed like an albatross. She huffed, scooted out of the booth, and picked up Ivy. "What kind of cereal do you want?"

I didn't like this new Emma, the responsible one. Although she fell into the role of my right-hand helper naturally, lately she never missed an opportunity to remind me of my failures. The air around us felt awkward at times.

Ivy settled on something fruity and sugar-loaded, adding another layer of guilt to my current mindset. I left them alone and went into the family room to sulk. A moment later, Grayson joined me on the sofa. He draped his arm around my shoulder and pulled me against him.

I wanted to cry but wouldn't. "I'm sorry she called you. I know you were busy."

He brushed his lips across my cheek. "Don't worry about it. I'm glad she thought to."

"Do you think it's anything I should be concerned about? The car in the driveway, I mean."

He turned and studied me. "I don't know. Should you?"

There hadn't been anything too controversial in the paper lately. Nothing worth paying me a home visit. Not everyone, irate readers especially, respected boundaries. Still, I didn't know the answer.

I pulled up the security system on my phone, keyed in the password, then chose the driveway camera. Luckily, I didn't need to scroll back too far. An image appeared but it wasn't clear. A thin layer of snow on the camera had melted and water streaked the lens. I brought the phone closer as if the action would clear away the water spots.

Grayson stared at the image with me. "It looks like a Land Rover."

Aaron? One, how does he know where I live? And two, why was he in my driveway?

CHAPTER 10

The roads were clear enough for school the next morning with an hour delay. I made sure Cole and Emma were up and ready before leaving for Doretha's with Ivy. Once there, she was in too much of a hurry to play with her friend Julian to let me take her coat off.

Doretha corralled the toddler and wrestled her out of the puffy jacket. "Wish I had an ounce of that energy."

The conversation with her brother was still fresh on my mind. "You got a minute?"

She cocked an unkept eyebrow. "Always for you. Coffee?"

I'd tolerate her thick, chicory-loaded coffee to pick her brain. "Sure."

I draped my own coat across the back of the kitchen chair then sat while Doretha fixed the coffee. She carried the mugs to the dinette table and sat across from me. Her braids and beads were pulled up into a scarf.

She stirred sugar into her cup, the spoon clanking against the side of the mug. It took her an unusual amount of time and I suspected she was waiting on me to speak first. That was her way. She'd offer advice when asked for.

"I saw Calvin yesterday. He asked me how Tommy was."

She jerked her eyes up and stared across the table. "Tommy?"

I nodded slowly. "Yeah. It made me wonder if, maybe, he needs to see a doctor."

"Bertie hadn't mentioned anything about something being wrong. Was Bertie there?"

"No. She'd gone to the store. And she left supper cooking on the stove for him to tend to."

Doretha took a drink of her coffee then waved me off. "If she left him tending to something on the stove, I'm sure he's fine." She nodded and a braid snaked its way out the confines of the scarf. "I talked to her just last week and she didn't say anything except that his sugar was better."

I sipped the coffee, accepting the bitterness in small amounts. "The whole conversation with him yesterday was strange. Even aside from the mention of Tommy."

"How so?"

"I was asking him about the mill and if there'd ever been any trouble when he worked there. It was like he was holding something back."

"What made you think that?"

"He avoided the direct questions. He'd skirt the issue and offer me tea or coffee, or anything really to change the subject."

"Well, maybe he really doesn't remember. You said he didn't remember about Tommy."

In theory, she had a point, but I knew what I saw. "No. He was perfectly lucid when we were talking about the mill. I told him I was asking the questions because of the remains we found. And then it was like someone pulled the blinds down."

"Like he didn't want to talk or didn't remember?"

"Like he didn't want to talk and was *pretending* not to remember."

Doretha smiled then chuckled. "Lord, child. Calvin's playing with you. Ain't you figured out how to tell when a man don't want to talk 'bout something?"

"So the whole Tommy thing...that was just a ruse?"

She chuckled still. Got up and topped off our coffee. "Probably."

But why? Calvin Lee Andrews knew something about those remains. He didn't fake those reactions. "He knows something, Doretha. I'm sure of it. You could see it in his face."

Doretha shook her head. Another braid escaped. "Calvin wouldn't be involved in anything like that."

"Of course he wouldn't. But he does know something."

She dumped a heaping spoonful of sugar in her coffee with no regard for her own diabetes. "Whatever Calvin knows, there's a reason he don't want to talk about it. So you best find another person to talk to."

"But why won't he talk about it?"

"It was a different time back then. A black man witnesses something he ain't supposed to see. You think he's gonna talk about it?"

That thought slammed me against a proverbial wall. I didn't see Calvin as a black man. I just saw him as a man. That's how it'd always been. I'd only read about the unrest sweeping the country at that time so thinking of Calvin, and Doretha, as suffering through it was foreign to me.

Doretha reached out and put her hand over mine. "Ava—if Calvin knows something, it must scare him. He may not feel safe talking about it."

"Even now? After all these years? What harm could come to

him?"

She sighed heavily and leaned back in her chair. "Remember the secret you and Grayson Ridge carried for so long? Terrified people would find out y'all was shacked up in a motel room when your husband was killed?"

Air hung in my lungs, refusing to move. Finally, I squeaked, "That's not fair. I was on the verge of leaving Tommy."

"But people didn't know that and y'all were scared of what people would think. Remember how long y'all kept that secret? And even now, I'm the only one who knows."

I shook my head. "What's that got to do with Calvin?"

"Whatever Calvin is holding on to, it's a secret and he wants to keep it that way."

"Even if it helps solve a murder?" My voice rose unintentionally.

She stared at me like she was trying to see inside me, trying to see something she had never seen. "You're not understanding, Ava."

"Then help me understand," I snapped.

"Calvin don't want no trouble. Simple as that. Didn't want it then and don't want it now."

"What am I supposed to do? Just ignore the fact he knows something about a murder?"

Doretha closed her eyes and sucked in a deep breath. She may have said a prayer. "Find another source. You're a reporter. You'll figure it out."

The fact was someone had died a violent death. Their body was buried without benefit of a casket. They deserved to have their story told. And the bottom line was—at least where my livelihood was concerned—a skeleton with a bullet in the skull was more of a story than rabbit hunting would ever be.

"I don't guess you'd talk to him for me?"

A tiny smile crept across her face. *"Child...."*

"He doesn't have to tell me. Just point me in the right direction."

"He did. You *know* something bad happened. Now find out why."

I finished my coffee then rinsed the mug out in the sink. Doretha was right—I was a reporter. I'd never been a crusader. There was no agenda for justice for John Doe. For all I knew, he might have been a horrible person.

Finding out who John Doe was would tell me why he died.

CHAPTER 11

If Calvin Lee Andrews wasn't going to talk, I'd focus on who the bones belonged to first, then piece together what happened later. Maybe by then he'd change his mind.

The office hummed with the usual day-before-press activity while Danny threatened to kill whoever made any more changes. Most of the requests were trivial on our end, but important to the readers. An ad client submitted the wrong coupon expiration date, a church added the wrong date in the events calendar, a Cub Scouts leader misspelled a kid's name in the photo caption, although that was one of mega importance— God hath no fury like that of a mother whose kid's name is spelled wrong in the paper.

With everything under control, I powered up my computer and dug further into the lives of Kelvin Dennis and Kenneth Dupree. I used Lexus-Nexis to connect the dots and form a timeline of Kelvin's life.

Last public activity was a credit report pulled in 2004. No big purchases followed. I went back to tax records from the house on Fisher Street he shared with his wife, Shelly. Recent records were in her name only. Kelvin's name disappears from public record after 2004. He even stopped getting arrested for assault on a female.

My radar went up. The back of my neck tickled like someone was whispering against my collar. Where was Kelvin Dennis? I switched programs and looked up Shelly Dennis to find a phone number, quickly jotted it down, then placed the call.

A woman answered on the third ring.

"May I speak to Shelly Dennis?"

The question was answered with silence before the woman cleared her throat. "Who is this?"

I identified myself and told her what I was calling for. "Have you got just a moment to talk?"

"I'm no longer married to Kelvin. I'm afraid I can't help you."

"How long have you been divorced?"

"Look, Miss...Logan, I haven't had anything to do with Kelvin for many years. I'm afraid I can't help you."

I wasn't giving up. "When's the last time you saw Kelvin?"

"I don't know. It was...years ago. At least thirteen."

I quickly did the mental math. "Is that how long you've been divorced?"

"We're not divorced."

That made no sense. "But you're no longer married to him?"

She huffed, seemingly resigned to the fact we were having this conversation. "I declared him dead five years ago."

I nearly choked on my coffee. *Declared dead?* Meaning no body was ever found. "I'd really like to talk with you in person if possible. Is it okay if I come by, say, within the next hour?"

"Miss Logan, I'd really—"

"We've found remains, Ms. Dennis."

Dead silence. Then I heard every breath. Finally, she shouted to someone in the background. When she returned to the call, she muttered, "I guess it's alright."

I confirmed the address then hung up. Why had Kelvin's name not shown up in public records that he was declared dead? Another search of his name provided the same results. Something wasn't adding up.

The coffee in the breakroom was strong but not bitter like Doretha's chicory. I filled my travel cup, hopeful that this road trip would be productive, then grabbed my bag on the way out. "Following a lead," I told Nola and anyone else interested.

Just as I reached it, the door opened and my hand landed square on Aaron Bell's chest. He took a step backwards. "Hello."

I backed him up then closed the door and faced off with him in the parking lot, shoving him again for good measure. I hadn't realized the anger inside until it started bubbling up and boiled like lava. I spit it out through clenched teeth. "Why the hell were you sitting in my driveway yesterday?"

He threw both hands up, either in defense or explanation, and stumbled backwards. I didn't care if he landed flat on his ass as long as he knew how pissed off I was. "I'm sorry—I really am," he stuttered.

"Why were you even there? You had no business being there." I struggled to keep my voice low so Nola and the crew wouldn't hear.

He scrambled for words as he regained his footing "I couldn't stop thinking about Mary McCarter, and what she did. I wanted to try to convince you to help me make the film."

"Yeah, well all it did was scare my kids half to death and that pissed me off. Don't ever do it again."

The guy looked traumatized. Eyes wide, cheeks pale. "I won't. I swear. When I saw that your car wasn't in the driveway, I didn't want to get out. I just sat there a minute then left."

It was more like fifteen minutes but who was counting? My ire was still up but it was settling into something non-violent. I brushed past him. "Just don't do it again. If I want you at my house, I'll invite you. Otherwise, stay off my property."

My hands were shaking when I climbed into the Tahoe. I seldom lost my temper but the surest way to piss me off was to mess with my kids. Aaron probably meant no harm, but he'd scared Emma enough to call Grayson. Who was I really mad at? Aaron for actually doing the responsible thing and leaving when he saw I wasn't home, or myself for failing to be there when Emma needed me? I punched Shelly's address in my phone and left Aaron standing in the parking lot.

Soon after, I turned onto Fisher Road. It was a winding trail in need of repaving, spotted with a farm or two and well-spaced houses with lawns that held up under the winter conditions. Shelly Dennis lived in a wood-sided cabin with a swing on the front porch. The place was nice. Well-kept. A flowerbed with the spiked remains of autumn mums lined the walkway to the house. Small patches of snow glistened in the shady spots. A newer model sedan sat parked beside a heavy-duty truck in the driveway.

Did both vehicles belong to Shelly?

She opened the door before I knocked. In jeans and a sweater, Shelly Dennis looked comfortable in her own skin. Chestnut hair that hadn't completely given in to gray was cut in a short bob. The only thing that stood out about her was the half-inch wide scar that ran along her neck from ear-to-ear. I pretended not to notice when she touched the ropey skin lightly with her fingertip. Was that a permanent gift from Kelvin? Like the suture scars running across my left knee like railroad tracks. Or the hairline fracture in my right shoulder. It's unseen, but it's there. A dull throb reminds me when it rains of being shoved against a rock fireplace.

She invited me in and I followed her into the kitchen. Heavy in the hips, she walked with a slight limp. Was that from age or another gift from Kelvin?

"We're just about to have a late breakfast. I hope you don't mind."

"No, not at all."

A man, solid build with salt and pepper hair, stood at the stove frying bacon. He was handsome in a plain sort of way. The kind to blend into a crowd. Much like Shelly herself, minus the Frankenstein scar. He gave a curt nod in my direction then went back to his cooking. Shelly made no effort to introduce him.

The kitchen opened into a family room with comfortable furniture and a ceiling fan spinning on low, spreading the smell of sizzling bacon.

Shelly sat at the table and motioned me toward one of the other seats. Despite the quaint feel of a pleasant home, unease hung in the air like the cloud of grease hovering over the stove. Although neither Shelly nor the man had been inhospitable, they didn't welcome me with open arms.

Shelly took a long draw off a vapor cigarette. "Would you like a cup of coffee?"

"No thank you."

"What do you want to know about Kelvin?"

There were several things that came to mind. Hopefully one answer would lead to another. "Do you mind if I take notes?"

She shook her head and sucked on the cigarette again.

I flipped to an empty page on my notepad. "Do you know what happened to him?"

She lifted one shoulder in a non-committed shrug. "Just disappeared one day. I was glad he was gone so I didn't ask too many questions."

"You haven't heard from him since?"

"Not a word." She fingered the scar at her neck. The constant reminder?

A lot of women would hide it behind a scarf. I admired that she wore it like a battle scar. In a sense, it was. "Did he do that?"

She nodded as she took another draw from the fake cigarette. "Yes. Last time I saw him."

My chest tightened with empathy. Tommy had never tried to kill me, but I could still relate. "I'm sorry."

Her companion placed a tray of bacon and toast on the table along with a bowl of scrambled eggs. Two plates and silverware followed. He sat beside Shelly then filled his plate. All without saying a word. I couldn't tell if he wasn't much of a talker or if he was holding his tongue. There was definitely an edginess surrounding him that made me uncomfortable

I plunged forward with the conversation whether he wanted to be part of it or not. "Have any family members been in contact with him?"

"Not that I know of." She shook the liquid in her vapor cigarette then stared at it like it was a misbehaving child.

"Does he have any family still alive?"

Shelly sighed impatiently. "Look, Miss Logan—Kelvin and I didn't have a great marriage. His family thought he was a saint and I was the evil witch. When I declared Kelvin dead, I said to hell with the rest of them, too." She shook the cigarette again then tossed it on the table.

"Did you have him declared *legally* dead?"

"I tried. Cost too much money. Money I didn't have at that time."

Her companion spread butter on a piece of toast like he was the only one in the room, oblivious to the conversation. He handed it to Shelly then buttered another for himself.

I pulled my attention off the silent third party. "What about his benefits? You could have collected—"

The silent third party suddenly spoke up. "Didn't want nothing from the sonofabitch."

Shelly patted his free hand with hers. "Martin gets upset when Kelvin's mentioned. As far as benefits, there wasn't any. Kelvin never worked a day in his life."

She seemed to battle back a sniffle. It could have been my imagination. Acknowledging a life she'd left behind with zero regrets would hardly bring tears.

"Do you know if any of his family is still living?"

Shelly scooped out some eggs then took a bite of bacon before answering. "His sister might be. Noreen Naylor. Last I heard she lived in West Jefferson."

A DNA sample would be worth the hour drive. I wrote the name down then returned the focus to the remains. "When did you and Kelvin start dating?"

"High school. Tenth grade."

"Were y'all in the same grade?" I didn't recall seeing Shelly in the yearbook.

"Both of us were the class of 1967. Jackson Creek High School."

I had gone back through the yearbook after finding their wedding announcement but never saw anyone named *Shelly*. At least not in the senior class. "Were you in the yearbook?"

"I was. In those god-awful cap and gown pictures."

I stared, trying to remember her face, trying to see her in a cap and gown.

After a long moment, she asked, "Is everything okay?"

I apologized, somewhat embarrassed. "I'm sorry. It's just I looked through the yearbook several times and don't recall seeing you. Or seeing anyone in the senior class named *Shelly*."

She shook the cigarette to get the liquid where it needed to be. "It wasn't under Shelly. School's the only place that went by my legal name."

"What *is* your legal name?"

"Michelle. Michelle Ann Myers."

KJD. And MAM.

CHAPTER 12

It wasn't often I got that adrenaline rush news people get when a secret is revealed. The *Jackson Creek Chronicle* seldom ran life shattering articles. But with this, the hair on my arms stood up.

"The last time you saw Kelvin—do you remember the date?"

She didn't hesitate. "March fourth, 2004."

"And that was the day he...cut you?"

She nodded, fingers massaging the scar. "Ear-to-ear. The surgeon said he missed the carotid by a quarter of an inch."

Martin snapped a strip of bacon in two and ate one of the pieces. He offered the other piece to Shelly.

"How long were you in the hospital?"

She nibbled on the end of the bacon. "Three weeks."

"And when you got out, was Kelvin gone?"

"Thank God," Martin mumbled. The man had yet to make eye contact with either me or Shelly.

Shelly reached over and patted his hand again. "Yes. He was gone."

"Had he taken his belongings?"

"I didn't notice anything missing. That's not to say he didn't...I just didn't notice. We didn't have a lot back then anyway. He never would work and it was hard on one salary."

"What about his clothes? Were they gone?"

"I didn't notice."

Like hell! If Tommy had slit my throat, I'd damn sure notice if there was any part of him still within striking distance.

"You have to understand what she went through," Martin said, meeting my eyes for the first time.

I did understand what she went through. I imagined the scene. Horror-filled and bloody. Had she screamed out until the shock set in? Tommy dislocated my shoulder twice, broke it once. The first time, the shock overshadowed the pain. After that, there was no shock. Only anger and lots of pain. Followed by a tearful apology from him. An explanation. How I'd just pushed the wrong button. My fault. Always my fault. Every bruise, every harsh word.

There was no way in hell I wouldn't notice that his clothes were gone.

I sucked in a deep breath and shoved away my own bad memories. Forcing myself to focus, I centered my thoughts on Kelvin. Did he feel remorse after each incident? Did he apologize and ask for forgiveness? Was there ever enough guilt to put a gun to his head and pull the trigger?

"Was Kelvin ever suicidal?"

Martin jerked his head up, his eyes now drilling through me. "Why would you ask that?"

I still didn't know the relationship between Martin and Shelly and didn't feel I owed him any explanation.

I turned back to Shelly. "Do you think Kelvin would have ever hurt himself?"

Martin spoke again. "Clearly you have a reason for asking that."

"To establish his frame of mind."

"The sonofabitch was crazy as a loon. That's all you need to know."

No, that wasn't all I needed to know and the more Martin protested, the more suspicious I became. Especially with the two of them not able to confirm if Kelvin had taken any of his belongings. That was hard to believe.

Shelly accepted the questioning better than Martin. Maybe it was something you had to live through to understand. She spoke softly, reminding me of my purpose of being there. "Miss Logan, you said on the phone that they'd found remains."

"Yes. All we know at this point is that they belong to a Caucasian male."

She took another hit off the vapor cigarette. "What makes you think it might be Kelvin?"

I hesitated in divulging too much. "The sheriff's department is following several leads right now. Sometimes it's easier to prove who it's not than to prove who it is."

"Process of elimination." Martin and I agreed on one thing.

"I still don't understand what led you to think it was Kelvin." Shelly said.

I dropped a few more breadcrumbs. "Something was found near the remains with initials."

I looked from one to the other as neither showed any surprise.

"Where were they found?" Martin said.

"The outskirts of town." I held back the details, though everyone would know when the paper hit the stands.

"Any idea how long they've been there?" Martin said.

"The remains are being tested. We'll know more when we get the results back. We do know the victim was probably between the ages of eighteen to twenty-five."

Although she had barely eaten, Shelly pushed her plate aside. "Kelvin was almost fifty the day he cut my throat. He was very much alive that day. Whether he was the next day, I can't say."

Would that be too much of an age variance to count Kelvin out? There were too many positives pointing in his direction to mark him off the list for now anyway.

"Why didn't you ever file a missing persons report on Kelvin?"

She shrugged. It was slight movement, tired, drained. "I didn't care if they never found him. I never wanted to hear his name again."

I understood the sentiment and didn't blame her at all. But the man didn't just stop existing even though he disappeared from her life. "What about what he did to you? Wasn't it reported as an assault?"

Domestic or not, the man had nearly killed her. There had to be some law enforcement involvement.

Martin spoke up. "The cops told her they were looking for him but after a few weeks, they moved on to other cases, I guess."

It happens. "Were you around back then?" I said to Martin.

Shelly smiled. "Martin's my brother, Miss Logan. He was around before I was born. He came to live with me after his wife died."

I saw the resemblance now. Same wide-set eyes, full lips. Could be anyone on the street.

Martin dropped more eggs on his plate. "I know what that man did to Shelly so there's no love lost here. If those remains are his, I say good riddance."

Did Martin hate him enough to kill him? How far would a brother go to revenge his sister? In these parts, they'd go as far as necessary.

Shelly lightly tapped the vapor cigarette on the table methodically. "You said there was an item found with the body with initials on it?"

"Yes. I went through the yearbook from 1967 and identified everyone with those initials."

Her mouth turned upward in the slightest of grins. Memories of simpler times, perhaps. I was certain there was a time she was giddy in love with Kelvin, just as I was with Tommy. "KJD and MAM," she said.

I didn't say yes or no. I didn't have to. She knew.

"He carved our initials in one of the picnic tables one time and the principal thought it was Kenny Dupree. Now that was a couple. Kenny and Mary."

"Mary?"

"Yeah, Mary. Everyone knew they'd get married. But from what I heard, he never came back from Vietnam."

I wrote "Mary" on my notepad. "Does Mary have a last name?"

"Mary McCarter."

CHAPTER 13

I sat in the Tahoe, hands shaking, heart pounding. Stunned, my chest ached as if someone had knocked the breath out of me. The eyes—those deep set eyes in that yearbook picture. I *knew* I had seen them before. They were the walking, talking, breathing embodiment of a simple-minded man named Keeper McCarter.

Mary had never named Keeper's father, but her son was a spittin' image of Kenneth James Dupree. I tried to do the math in my head but wasn't sure of Keeper's age. I had an estimate, but all that did was lead to assumptions.

The revelation was stunning, no doubt about that. But there was still a dead John Doe. And Kenneth James Dupree never came home from Vietnam. I settled my thoughts and stilled the shaking, then shifted focus back to Kelvin Dennis.

A Google search on my phone for a Noreen Naylor in West Jefferson brought up one entry. A Facebook profile. I logged in through the paper's account then typed her name in the search bar. The screen filled with images of recipes, kittens and bible verses. She worked in the deli at Walmart. I found the link to the megastore, copied the phone number for the deli, and dialed.

After a couple rings, someone finally picked up. "Deli. How

can I help you?"

I set the GPS for the store. "May I speak to Noreen Naylor?"

"Yeah, hold on. Noreen..."

That was all I needed to know. I disconnected the call and headed to West Jefferson. The drive would give me time to put my thoughts into order and come up with an introduction. Ambushing people for a story wasn't my style but this had gone beyond the article. It had become a mission. I couldn't shake the grotesque image of the necklace Shelly was sentenced to wear the rest of her life. If the remains were Kelvin's, I wasn't sure how I'd handle that. Part of me would shed sympathy for the fact there was no funeral, no acknowledgement of his death. The other part would spit on him.

Did he deserve what he got? I'd save judgement until I had the whole story.

I called Grayson. After filling him in on my visit with Shelly, I asked if there were any new developments on his end.

"Felicia's got a colleague working on a facial reconstruction made out of gypsum. I didn't want to release the skull. Not with a slug still in it."

Made sense. "If Kelvin's sister is willing, can we do a DNA comparison?"

Slow to answer, he finally sighed. "I'll consider it."

"*Consider it*? It's the only lead on an identity we have." My voice inched upward.

"Identifying the remains is just the first step. After that, I'm investigating a murder and that evidence has to hold up in court."

In other words, the sheriff's department will conduct the *official* investigation. Which meant the open communication would stop. I'd do my job and he'd do his and the less they crossed paths, the better. I took a deep breath. Reminded myself I loved him.

The frustrating part was I got it. I understood. Our jobs didn't always work well together. I wasn't on the sheriff's department payroll and he wasn't on mine. So I changed the subject. "Aaron Bell came by the office this morning." I gave him a recap of mine and Aaron's meeting in the parking lot.

"Do you believe him?"

After thinking about it a moment, I said, "I don't really have a reason not to."

"Are you going to help with the film?"

"I haven't decided. I haven't had time to watch the one about Vietnam yet."

"Maybe we can do that tonight after the kids go to bed."

The statement sent warm fuzzies through me, making me forget all about the conflict our jobs created. *The* kids. Not *your* kids. I smiled. "Sounds like a plan."

"We have a date, Miss Logan. I'll send you a picture of the facial reconstruction as soon as I can get it."

After chatting another minute or two, we hung up. I did love him, dearly. Our jobs got in the way sometimes, but so far, we'd never had a deal breaker.

The streets were clear of dirt-filled snow in West Jefferson. Still, the winter gloom enveloped the small town like an obnoxious neighbor who had overstayed their welcome. The Christmas tree farms provided hot chocolate and joy during the holiday season. After that, the weekend skiers found their joy on the nearby slopes. But after that, in the lull between the holidays and warmer weather, this part of western North Carolina spent the weeks looking forward to the next day when we were that much closer to spring.

The megastore anchored a shopping center with a few smaller shops and chain restaurants. Besides offering groceries, housewares, and oil changes, it also offered jobs. They weren't top-paying positions with CEO potential, but it was gainful employment and that's what the people needed. Trying to outrun welfare was better than having it catch up to you.

The parking lot was an assortment of trucks, SUVs and second-hand cars. Some still carried the signage of a winter storm with ashy-looking tires and running boards. Despite temperatures close to forty degrees, the wind bit at my cheeks. I turned my face into my scarf and hurried inside. Rubber floor mats with remnants of snow and de-icer from winter boots were spread out at the automatic doors.

Laid out like the store at home, the deli and bakery were to the left. I smiled at the greeter then headed for the counter. Two women chatted behind the glass cases as they filled the stainless steel bins. Hair pulled up in hairnets, gloves on their hands, and nametags.

Noreen appeared the older of the two. The crow's feet framing her eyes matched the lines etched deep into her cheeks. She looked up at me as she scooped pasta salad from an industrial sized tub into the bin. "Can we help you?"

I introduced myself. "I'm with the *Jackson Creek Chronicle*. I was wondering if I might talk with you in private for just a moment?"

"Oh, I've seen that paper," Noreen said. "Pick it up every time I'm up that way."

The younger one laughed. "You might be in the paper, Noreen."

Smiling, Noreen waved her off. "I can take my break now I guess. Give me just a second."

She put the tub away then tossed her gloves into the trash. The other woman kept a watchful eye on me. Protecting her co-worker. Or being nosey, most likely. Anticipating Noreen's five minutes of fame courtesy of the newspaper.

Noreen stepped around the counter and headed toward the instore cafe. She walked with a waddle, like it hurt to put pressure on aching feet. "Mind if we go sit down?"

I followed her to a two-seater table. She waved at the girl at the register, asked how her mother was doing. The cashier called her "Miss Noreen" and asked if she wanted her usual. She then brought over a small coffee and one pink pack of fake sugar. The girl asked if I wanted anything and I ordered a coffee, too.

Shortly after, the waitress brought over mine.

Noreen gently blew into her cup. "What can I do for you, Miss Logan?"

This poor sweet lady seemed so nice, I couldn't imagine her thinking bad about anyone like Shelly had claimed. Noreen looked the kind to offer a prayer for whatever the situation.

I carefully broached the subject of her brother. "I was hoping you could shed some light about your brother's disappearance."

She blinked several times. "Kelvin?"

"Yes. When was the last time you saw him?"

More puffs of soft breath in her coffee to stall. The drink had already lost its steam. "It's been quite a while. Years, I guess."

"It's important to narrow it down as close as you can."

"They've found a body, haven't they?" Dampness collected in her eyes. She blinked again until it spilled out and trickled down her cheek.

"The sheriff's department is still in the early stages of their investigation, so nothing has been confirmed."

Everything I'd thought earlier, of spitting on Kelvin's remains, smacked me in the face. Even if he wasn't worthy of anyone else's love, his younger sister, Noreen, did love him. I wondered about their childhood. Was he the big brother many young girls in that era wanted? The protector? Or was he a tormentor?

"We're just chasing down leads right now. We're trying to establish a timeline to help determine an identity."

She nodded. Sipped her coffee. "The last time I saw him was, I guess back in 2001. He showed up at Uncle Finch's funeral. I'm pretty sure it was 2001. I'd have to go back and look at the obituary."

The exact date didn't really matter. He was very much alive when he cut Shelly's throat in 2004. If it was 2001 or there about when Noreen saw him last, they must not have had a close relationship. Four years plus of not seeing one another? Understandable if they lived states away. But one county over?

"You and Kelvin didn't see each other very often?"

She stared into her coffee and shook her head. "After I got married and moved away, I hardly ever saw him. He wasn't real close to anyone. He was that way. Kelvin had his share of problems." She looked up and wiped her face with the back of her age-spotted hand. "Have you talked to Shelly?"

"Yes. Shelly's the one who gave me your name."

She nodded, sniffled, then squared her shoulders. "If something happened to him, that's who you need to be looking at."

I had Shelly and her brother on my list.

I understood Noreen's slow burn of anger, simmering all these years, but Shelly was fighting for her life when Kelvin left.

"Shelly was hospitalized when he disappeared, Noreen. The last time she saw him was when he cut her throat."

She flinched at the ugly truth. Looking away then finally settling her gaze at her trembling hands. "I'd heard she was in the hospital. They seemed to fight a lot."

I wanted to tell her I'd seen the scar and it was real. It was deep and ugly and still pink after all these years. But she knew that. She knew what her brother had been capable of.

"Do y'all have any other family he might have kept in touch with?"

"Not really. Momma died eight years ago, and Daddy died when we were teenagers."

"Did he ever contact your mother when she was living?"

She slowly shook her head. "Not that I know of. She had Alzheimer's so she may not have even remembered him if he had contacted her."

"I'm sorry." It seemed like the right thing to say, and it was heartfelt. As happy as Noreen seemed on the outside, there was a fair amount of sadness buried behind the cheerful smile.

"Probably for the best anyway. It'd have broken her heart knowing what he turned out to be. My daddy wasn't a nice man, either." She glanced at me, then turned away, embarrassed for her father's dirty deeds.

Round and round the circle went. "He hit your mother?"

She jerked her head up and down, a spastic nod, like she was hoping the quicker she admitted it, the quicker it would go away. It didn't work like that and deep down, I'm sure she knew.

"At least Kelvin got it honestly, right?"

I didn't say anything. I understood her pain and the shame that came with it.

Noreen finished her coffee then tapped the empty cup on

the table while she gathered her thoughts. "We did have a cousin he'd pal around with sometimes. But I haven't talked to him in years so...I don't know if they stayed in touch."

Did no one in the Dennis family keep in touch? A Christmas card? Family reunion? Or was it just Kelvin everyone avoided? "What's the cousin's name?"

"Grant Dennis. I think he was living near Bristol last I heard."

I typed his name into the Notes app on my phone. "Do you mind if I give you a call if I have more questions?"

"I guess that would be ok." She gave me her cell number, then said, "Will you call when they identify the body? It would set my mind at ease, knowing for sure."

"Of course. I'll give you a call one way or the other. Would you be willing to submit to a DNA test?" Grayson wasn't too enthusiastic about it when I mentioned it but at least I'd set the groundwork if Noreen was interested.

Her teary eyes widened like I'd asked her to donate a kidney. "What all's involved in that? I don't get a lot of time off from work."

Self-preservation overshadowed the need to know what happened to her brother. "It's a simple test. Actually, they can probably pull it from your coffee cup. Do you mind if I take it with me?" The faint pink lipstick smudge around the rim would work just fine.

She shrugged, eyebrows scrunched. "The wonders of science, huh." She stood and smoothed her blue smock. "I've got to get back to work. If you do find out anything, please let know."

"I will. Just keep in mind these tests can take months, even years."

"I understand. What's another year, right?" As she started to limp away, a statement she'd made sprang to mind. "Noreen—you said if something had happened to Kelvin, Shelly was who I needed to talk to. What did you mean by that?"

"Not Shelly. That brother of hers. No amount of prayer can fix him."

Martin struck me as being on the odd side. But to what extent? Enough to kill his brother-in-law? Who was protecting who in his relationship with Shelly? I didn't want to judge Shelly too harshly—she had that necklace justifying some of her actions. Not all. But some.

Noreen headed back to the deli. I asked the cashier in the café for a to-go bag for Noreen's discarded cup. She scrambled to get a bag for me with trembling hands. "I'm sorry. I couldn't help but overhear."

Eavesdrop was more like it. After dropping the cup in the white paper sack, I thanked the girl with a smile.

The girl leaned into the counter and whispered, "You really think Noreen's brother was murdered?"

"Um...no. We have no reason to believe that," I lied. "Thanks for the bag."

I gave her another smile then got out of there before she could ask another question. Guaranteed before I could get out to the Tahoe that word would spread through the store about Noreen's brother's brutal murder. It may not be far from the truth.

Just as I cranked the engine, my cell beeped with an incoming text from Grayson.

You need to see this facial reconstruction. Hurry back.

CHAPTER 14

I texted Grayson but didn't get a reply. I called and it went to voicemail. At least we were back to sharing information. When I arrived, I parked beside his Expedition at the sheriff's department and rushed inside, gripping the paper bag with Noreen's coffee cup. Hopefully, there'd be no need to pull the DNA. But I was prepared if there was, whether Grayson wanted to acknowledge it or not.

The offices and a makeshift holding cell were in an old turn-of-the-century bank, complete with a marble teller counter that was now Grayson's secretary's desk. Annie had served under so many sheriffs it was understood that she came with the job. She was secretary to the sheriff before Grayson was born and never let him forget it.

Despite being perched behind the raised counter, she was tiny. She seemed to shrink a little more each year. A little more stooped, a little more hair turned white. A little more "don't give a shit" attitude, too. She'd wear her blood red lipstick if she wanted to, even if it feathered around her thinning lips. Glancing up over the counter, she smiled when I came in. "He's in his office."

Anxious to see the picture, I didn't stop to give Annie a hug. Just smiled back and hurried down the hall. His office door was open so I didn't miss a stride. Dr. Scranton was beside him at his desk, leaning over and pointing at the computer monitor. In jeans and a bulky sweater, flaming red hair pulled back into a ponytail, she looked more like a teenager than someone with a PhD. The splash of freckles across the bridge of her nose didn't add to her age either.

She looked up over her glasses and I swear she frowned. Full, pouty lips pursed tight into a scowl. Was she pissed I was there? Didn't matter. Grayson had asked me to come see the picture and had even added *hurry back*.

"You ready for this?" He waved me over then turned the monitor so I could see.

A jolt grabbed my chest and squeezed like a vice. I blinked several times as I stared at the image. It was a heart-stopping likeness of Keeper McCarter. My mind scrambled to the picture of Kenneth Dupree in the yearbook, to what Shelly had said about Kenneth and Mary. This looked just like his picture in the yearbook minus the dark curls.

My words came in a breathless whisper. "Oh my God."

"It's not even finished yet," Grayson said. "This is just the preliminary."

"She still has to add the muscle tone around the jaw line," Dr. Scranton added.

I pulled a chair up closer to the desk and continued to stare at the image. "It's incredible."

It was like looking at a bare-boned version of Keeper. But Kenneth Dupree never came back from Vietnam. There was no way the remains belonged to Dupree.

"What do you know about Mary's family?" Grayson asked.

I thought about it for a minute then told him as much as I knew. "Her father died a few years ago of cancer. I went to the funeral and watched them put him in the ground, so I know that's not him. I don't know much about her mother. She has a brother, Roy. He lives in a trailer on the property. Helps out some on the farm, I think, when he's not tipping a bottle. And then of course there's Keeper."

I shared what Shelly Dennis had told me about Dupree and Mary. "The initials do match those on the ring. But Kenneth Dupree never came back from the war, he might be Keeper's father, but—" I pointed to the screen. "That can't be him."

Grayson cocked an eyebrow. "Do we know for sure Dupree is Keeper's father?"

He was right. Even if Mary had been in a relationship with Kenneth Dupree, it didn't mean he and Keeper were father and son. I pointed at the screen. "But that's nearly identical to Dupree's picture in the yearbook. That *has to be* Kenny Dupree."

But Kenny never came home from the war. Or did he?

A vision of Mary nearly collapsing earlier crept into my memory. She had felt a connection to the skeletal body through me. Would it have been strong enough to knock her off her feet if Keeper wasn't the link? I'd been around her before when she'd had a vision or experienced an aura, but never like that. Never one so intense.

"I don't know who these people are you're talking about," Dr. Scranton said, "but if we could get a DNA sample from one of them it might be helpful."

Now she wanted to include me? I pushed aside the brewing animosity for the sake of Mary McCarter. "I'll ask Mary."

I asked Grayson to print the picture for me. Maybe if I took it with me, Mary would be more apt to talk. More open about her past. It would be hard to deny the resemblance when it was staring back at you.

Grayson checked the printer on the credenza behind him for paper, added a small stack then hit print. "What'd you find out in West Jefferson?"

I waved the paper bag with the discarded coffee cup. "I got a used paper cup for DNA comparison. But it was all kinda weird."

He handed me two copies of the picture of our John Doe. "Weird how?"

"The family. It was just so fractured. I mean Noreen hasn't talked to her brother in well over a decade. Has no idea what ever happened to him. She gave me the name of a cousin he used to hang out with who she *thinks* lives in Bristol."

He looked thoughtful, like he was searching his own memories. "Parents still alive?"

"No and mother had Alzheimer's so she wouldn't have remembered anything anyway."

Grayson came from a family of seven kids. With four brothers and two sisters, enough nephews and nieces to field any sports team, not to mention uncles and aunts, small family dynamics were foreign to him.

I was an only child until I went to live with Doretha. Foster kids aren't bound by blood but by circumstance. As adults, we don't see each other every day, and sometimes that stretched into months, but we always knew how to get in touch. Shared the major milestones right along with the tragedies. I've often wondered if my parents had been somewhat functional and had more children, if we would have stayed together when our home life imploded.

Dr. Scranton frowned again, something she seemed to do

often. "And how does West Jefferson relate to John Doe?"

I explained the connection of how I'd come up with the names Kelvin Dennis and Kenneth Dupree, again. Maybe she'd discarded our earlier conversations as non-essential?

She stared at me, still frowning, and I decided it was her natural expression. Some people seem to smile all the time. Not her. She nodded slightly. She pointed to the computer screen where the facial reconstruction stared at us. "And this one looks like Dupree?"

"Yeah, but Dupree never came back from Vietnam."

"Killed or missing?"

I shrugged. "Presumed missing. His parents said the last they heard from him was in July of '69. He told them his tour was up and he was coming home but never showed. The army said he probably never left Southeast Asia."

Everyone thought on that for a moment then Grayson said, "Any chance his parents are still alive?"

"I found the obituary for his father but nothing on his mother. He had a sister and a brother, both are still living."

"What about the other guy?" Dr. Scranton asked.

"Kelvin Dennis seemed to have disappeared off the face of the earth. He's not in any public record after 2004. The last time we've got an exact date on his whereabouts is March 2004 when he cut his wife's throat."

Grayson lifted his eyes to meet mine. "Nice guy. No arrest?"

"No. There may still be an open warrant for him, I don't know. It didn't show up."

Grayson wrote the name down followed by "March 2004." Dr. Scranton watched him then turned her crunched little nose up in my direction. "You're very resourceful. I've never seen the media and the law enforcement work so closely."

She'd said that a couple times already. A little overkill if you asked me.

"It's not standard but we make it work." Grayson gave me a wink.

The tiny action smoothed my ruffled feathers and I smiled. "Yes, we do. I'm going to see Mary now, but are we still going to watch Aaron's documentary tonight?"

He nodded. "I'd like to see his work."

I stood there for a minute contemplating whether or not to kiss him goodbye. Decided I'd pushed the envelope far enough for today, gathered the paper bag and pictures and started to leave.

"You want to leave the cup?" Grayson said.

I hesitated. I actually *hesitated*. What had changed since I asked him about getting a DNA sample from Noreen Naylor earlier? When he gave me the spiel about evidence holding up in court? Nothing except we now had damn good reason to believe the bones did not belong to Kelvin Dennis. Did he even have any intention of testing it?

"You're not going to toss it, are you?" I said, only half joking but handed it to him anyway.

"Going to log it in and store it. Even if these remains aren't Kelvin Dennis, he's out there somewhere."

He wrote "Noreen Naylor" and the date on the bag with a Sharpie. "Let me know what Mary says."

"Yeah. I will." I took the pictures and headed to the Tahoe, again not stopping to give Annie a hug. She called "bye" to me on my way out and I gave her a wave over my shoulder.

I climbed in the SUV and sat there in the cold. One minute he strictly abided by the rules of the job, the next minute he encouraged my participation in the investigation. "Make up your damn mind, Grayson," I mumbled then cranked the engine.

There was still one piece of the puzzle I hadn't shared with him yet. Calvin Lee Andrews. I'd keep that piece to myself for the time being. After talking with Doretha, I didn't want to drag Calvin into something he wanted no part of. Unless it became necessary.

CHAPTER 15

I brushed off the feeling of not really knowing *what* I was feeling. It wasn't anger. Not toward Grayson, anyway. Or maybe it was. We worked well together and I'd never questioned the guarded aspects of an investigation. Nor had he ever had to remind me what was off the record. But with this one, there was a tiny sprout of discontent edging its way between us. And maybe that tiny sprout spreading the discontent was a spunky redhead?

"*Stop it,*" I said out loud. We'd worked through a tough investigation before. We'd do it again.

My bigger concern was how was I going to broach the subject of Keeper's parentage with Mary. Truthfully, it was no one's business. Unless the remains were Kenneth Dupree's. That was a whole different ballgame. I'd cross that bridge if and when we got to it.

I pushed the thoughts to the far corners of my brain and concentrated on the twists and turns of the road. The switchbacks in this part were awful with dented guardrails as evidence. When I got to Mary's, I sat in the driveway and collected my thoughts. My mind kept flashing back to Mary nearly collapsing in my arms when she experienced the vision. What in God's name would this do to her?

The curtain in the living room pulled back a tad, just enough for someone to see who was in the driveway. I took another look at the picture, then at Keeper as he stepped out onto the porch. He waved excitedly and warmth spread through my soul like water trickling through a stream, slow and easy. I loved these people so much. Knowing I had information that may hurt them weighed heavy on my chest. I dropped the picture in my bag then walked up the drive to greet him.

He wrapped his arms around me and squeezed out a hug like he hadn't seen me in years. "Hey Ava! Momma, Ava's here. Where's your friend?"

"Aaron? I'm not sure where he is today." I knew where *he* best not be and that was my driveway.

Keeper shuffled me inside then closed the door behind us. Mary sat on the sofa with stacks of clean laundry on the cushion beside her. She pulled fresh-smelling garments from a plastic basket, carefully folding each one.

"Look, Momma. Ava's here."

Mary smiled that tiny smile of hers then moved a stack of clothes from the sofa. She patted the empty cushion. "I can see that, Son. Here, Ava, have a seat."

I sat beside Mary while Keeper curled into an old recliner in front of a modest television, entranced by an afternoon game show.

I'd never given much thought to their living room as most of the time, Mary was in the kitchen brewing up some new tonic when I visited. The room was dated with green and brown plaid furniture older than me. A large dreamcatcher hung in a corner like a mobile over a baby's crib. Gold-plated picture frames, some showing signs of tarnish, hung in no specific pattern over the sofa. Others sat propped on the mantel. Mary's parents, just married in one and celebrating an anniversary in another. Mary and Roy as kids, bare-kneed with dirty feet. The majority, by far, were of Keeper. From a fat little baby in cloth diapers to a slim kid with too-short jeans that had holes in the knees. The last one, at least the most recent one that was framed and on display, was of Keeper a few years ago in an ill-fitting suit. It was the day of his grandfather's funeral. I remembered the day, the suit and how Keeper kept pulling and tugging on it and how Mary kept brushing his hand away, telling him he was handsome.

"How's your friend, Aaron?" Mary said.

I figured I'd spare her the details of our near parking lot brawl. "He's much better. No pain or blistering."

Mary put the last stack of laundry back into the basket. "That's good. What can I do for you?"

I spoke softly, allowing the television show's emcee to bury my words. "Can we talk privately?"

Immediately, she glanced at her son. "I could use a cup of tea. Come on in the kitchen."

Keeper was so involved in the game show he didn't notice when we left the room. Mary put the kettle on the stove then took down two mugs from the cupboard. "Peppermint okay?"

"Sounds great." Though, I wanted Kava or some Chamomile to calm my nerves.

She turned around and leaned against the counter, waiting on the kettle to rattle its shrill alarm. She folded her hands in front. "So are you going to tell me why you're here? You're as jumpy as a catfish on land."

Funny how she noticed. I thought I'd concealed it better. I

stopped tapping my feet and drew in a deep breath. Hesitantly, I took the picture out of my bag but didn't open it. I laid it on the table, still closed. "The remains that were found earlier in the week—we have a partial facial reconstruction."

The kettle gurgled then screeched. For a moment, Mary lingered and let the water boil until it became an ear-shattering scream. She finally lifted the kettle off the stove then poured the boiling water into the two mugs. She carried both mugs to the table then sat across from me. "I thought all that scientific stuff took a lot longer."

"It normally does. I guess we just lucked out this time. And it is just a partial. They still need to add to it." I drank the tea even though it was scalding hot. Searing pain pierced my tongue but I refused to give into it. It was a welcome distraction from my jumpy nerves.

Mary sipper her tea, unfazed. "Is it anybody you recognize?"

Hesitating, I slowly slid the paper across the table to her. Although it was still closed, she stared at it like she already knew who it was. Maybe she did.

She quickly opened the folded paper. Tears immediately dampened her eyes as she turned the paper over, seeing all she needed to see. "It's not possible," she whispered.

"Is this Keeper's father?" I kept my voice low, praying he'd remain more interested in the game show than what his momma and I were doing.

She shook her head in a jerky motion then brushed a tear away from her cheek. "It can't be. That's not Kenny, Ava. It can't be. He died in the war."

I tapped the picture. "Is *this* Kenny?"

"It looks like him. But Kenny never came home. Those

remains can't be his. He did have a younger brother who looked a lot like him. His name was Russell." Her voice was as shaky as her hands. She sucked on her bottom lip to hold back the emotional tidal wave that threatened to spill at any time.

"There was a class ring found with the body. Class of '67. The initials KJD and MAM were engraved in it."

A tiny gasp followed by a quick look away. Painfully searching through decades-old memories. The confusion of years of unanswered questions bore down hard on her face.

My own heart broke for her. "Did anyone know Kenny was Keeper's Daddy?"

She shook her head and took a long, deep breath. Held her hands out in front, fingers laced, nerves racing. "I know there was a lot of talk, a lot of rumors. One look at my son, and it didn't take much to put it together. Girls back then who were in my situation usually got sent away to a distant aunt's house or even a girl's home. The baby was usually put up for adoption and no one ever mentioned it again."

"But you didn't do that with Keeper. Why?"

She stared into her tea as if seeing her past rather than reading her future. "Kenny and I were going to get married when he came home from the war. We were going to buy a little piece of land and raise our baby. But he never came home."

I reached out and covered her hands with mine, a little surprised there wasn't a jolt of electricity with it. "Did you remain in touch with his family?"

"His father contacted me to see if Kenny had been in touch after he was discharged."

"Had he?"

Her eyes watered again but she squeezed them closed, defiantly shaking her head. "I didn't even know he'd been discharged."

Mary pushed out of her chair and walked over to the counter, clearly remembering something she didn't want to. She took a stem of an herb and began gently pulling tiny leaves away from the stalk. Anything to keep busy.

From the living room, Keeper roared with laughter at the game show. He clapped with exuberant enthusiasm. Mary stopped plucking the herb for a moment and cocked her head toward the living room, smiling. "He loves those game shows. He and Daddy used to watch them together."

Probably some of the same shows playing in the background of my own childhood. I pushed aside the pleasant memories to dredge back up something Mary was clearly trying to avoid. "Kenny never told you he was being discharged?"

"I made all kinds of excuses. Like young girl's in love will do. But, yeah—the bottom line was not long after we talked about getting married, raising our baby...I stopped hearing from him. Can't tell you how many letters I wrote that were never answered."

"I'm sorry." And I was. I could imagine the pain. A broken heart hurts no matter the age. The numbness followed by that burning in the center of your chest. Nothing in the world could hurt as bad.

She lifted her shoulders in a shrug. Sniffled back tears. "It happens. I wasn't the first teenager to get herself pregnant by a boy she thought loved her."

"Did you tell his family?"

"No. No one thought the relationship was serious. Everyone chalked it up to one of those *teenage things,* I guess. Nothing serious. Or so they thought. Maybe it wasn't..." Her voice trailed off, shrouded in memories.

"They don't know about Keeper?"

She shook her head and spoke in a soft voice. "They'd already moved when I found out I was pregnant. Kenny was already overseas."

They had a grandson they never knew about. A living link to their own son. "Did you ever think about reaching out to them? Telling them about Keeper?"

Mary finished with that stem and tossed the leftovers in the compost pail. Reaching for another stem, she hesitated then sighed heavily. "I was scared they'd try to take him from me. Especially when Kenny didn't come back."

An unmarried seventeen-year-old with a handicapped child? Her fear was justified. "Were they wealthy?"

"Not really, but they weren't farm poor either." She left the new herb laying on the cutting board and came back over to the table to reclaim her seat. "You have to understand, I'd only met his parents one time. Kenny introduced us at graduation."

"What about your parents? Did they want to send you away and give up the baby?"

She chuckled. It was a slight sound, barely audible. "Momma was sick by then, so I was needed at home. Only way I got to keep my baby was because my momma was dying and I had to take care of her. Wasn't old enough to take care of a baby, but I was sure old enough to change my momma's diaper."

Back then there were few other options. Assisted living didn't exist in these mountains. Nursing homes were a half-day's drive and required a rich man's salary. There were no home care nurses or hospice or pay-by-the-hour adult sitters. There was family. And most often the family member assigned the task of taking care of Momma or Daddy was the daughter. It wasn't fair. But that's just the way it was.

Keeper guffawed from the living room then hollered to Mary that she ought to see this person's hat. *Let's Make a Deal*, maybe? I bet he did enjoy that one.

"What now?" Mary asked. "Where do we go from here?"

I wish I knew. She was hell-bent that the remains weren't Kenny Dupree, yet the facial reconstruction—only partially finished—was either him or his doppelganger. And what if it was him? That raised almost as many questions as the skeletal remains themselves.

"We'll keep piecing together the puzzle," I said for lack of a better answer.

"Well, I do hope you can identify the remains. I'm sure there's a family wanting to know what happened."

I opened the picture again and took another look at it, more certain now than before it was Kenny Dupree. Even if Mary didn't want to admit it.

CHAPTER 16

I stood in my family room staring out the windows, watching the leftover snow glisten in the moonlight on the river bank. The kids were already in bed, cocooned in the safety of home and family. Grayson fiddled with the television, trying to get the right source to watch Aaron's documentary on veterans called *Easter's Promise.* I couldn't help but think of Mary and the pain she'd suffered. Not knowing was harder than the truth. Even when it stared back at you from a picture. What would it take to convince her the remains were Kenny Dupree's? If they were. I still had doubts myself. There was no proof he ever returned from overseas. So how could he end up with a bullet in his head at the old mill? Unless, Kenny Dupree wasn't Keeper's father? Could that be possible?

"How long before we get the DNA back from the remains?" I moved away from the windows and joined Grayson on the couch. I curled into him, feeling secure within the realm of my little world.

"Felicia's got a rush on it. Maybe a few days."

He draped one arm around my shoulder and pulled me closer. I felt safe in his strength. "Mary doesn't want to believe it's Kenny Dupree."

"The picture looks just like Keeper. She can't deny that."

"No, but Kenny Dupree never came home from Vietnam."

"According to Mary."

That statement jarred me. I pulled away just enough to look him in the eye. "You can't think Mary had something to do with it?"

"Probably not. But we do have to consider *everything*."

He pressed the play button on the remote and settled in for the film. I let the first few minutes roll by without paying much attention. Mary McCarter occupied my thoughts.

After a few minutes, the documentary tugged my focus. The style was impressive with breathtaking cinematography. The story focused on a woman in the Piedmont region who founded and ran a therapeutic equine center for wounded veterans. The center was named after the director's first horse, Easter. The name itself was a promise of new beginnings. Being around horses, whether riding, brushing or just general care, had proven beneficial to those suffering with PTSD. Aaron had brilliantly captured the woman's passion toward the center. The veterans interviewed were a jambalaya of branches of service, wars fought in, and wounds—visible and unseen. The horses accepted the warriors no matter what ailed them.

I watched the two guys from the Vietnam era with a new interest. Black and white snapshots of young men, kids really, in their combat gear, cigarettes dangling from unshaven faces. Smiles hiding the suffering of war, the horrors they'd witnessed. I wondered what it was about those jungles that would make someone give up their family, their life here, to stay in a place that had been so hostile to them? Was Kenny Dupree alive and well and living on a beach in Thailand? Or was he shot to death right here in his own backyard?

All in all, I was impressed by the way Aaron handled the subject matter. It was gentle, non-confrontational, and thoughtful. Richly produced with award-worthy cinematography. Although the war was before my time, I knew through history Vietnam veterans were often misrepresented, just like the people of Appalachia. We were no more all a bunch of toothless hillbillies than they were all baby-killers. The clichés that bound the two demographics gave me a soft spot for the truth and inched me toward agreeing to help him. But I still didn't like him in my driveway uninvited.

After the film ended, Grayson shut down the television and closed the doors to the fireplace while I let Finn and Boone out one more time before heading to bed. I gathered up the empty pizza box from supper and carried it outside to the fire pit. The air was biting with a damp coldness, snow still covering the ground in spots.

The security spotlights flickered on, lighting up the whole backyard. Just as I tossed the box onto the charred discards, ashes puffed around it, revealing a shiny, yet half-burned condom wrapper.

I couldn't look away. I must have stared at it for several minutes with every thought imaginable running through my mind. Silver wrapper. The brand Grayson and I used. The kind that was tucked away in the drawer of the nightstand on his side of the bed.

But we didn't burn bathroom trash. That went in the huge trash can we dragged to the side of the road once a week. So why was it in the fire pit?

I lowered myself onto one of the benches surrounding the pit and continued to stare at it. Did Grayson give it to him? My

son had lied to me. Did Emma know? God, I hoped Emma
didn't know. I wasn't ready for *that* conversation.

Lost in confused thoughts, I didn't hear Grayson come up
behind me. "What are you doing? It's freezing out here." He
leaned over the bench and wrapped me in his arms. "You okay?"

I shook my head. "Not really." I pointed to the wrapper
gleaming amongst the ashes.

Grayson came around and sat beside me. He sighed heavily
enough that I heard it. "You knew it was going to happen sooner
or later."

"I would have preferred later. Much later."

"Honey, he's sixteen. He's a walking hormone. At least he
thought enough to use protection."

I shoved my hair behind my ears, not buying the good news
aspect. It would take a lot more to convince me I should be
proud of my son's "good" judgement.

"Did he take that from your stash?" I said.

"Well, I don't think they come with serial numbers on them
so there's no way to tell for sure. But if I had to bet...."

"That means he went through our nightstand drawers."

"Shit." Grayson rarely cursed. I was the one with the gutter
mouth when riled so hearing it come from him was weird.

Not nearly as weird as the thought of everything in that
drawer. Velvet-lined handcuffs. Vibrator. All kinds of gels and
edible oils. There might have even been a silk blindfold.

Grayson was the first one to giggle. Damn him. This was a
serious moment. How was I supposed to be Supermom if I
laughed at knowing my son was now sexually active? Or with the
humiliation that came from knowing your son had probably
discovered *your* toys?

"It's really not funny," I said between chuckles.

"You're right. It's hilarious."

"Do I let him know I know?"

"Are you prepared to hear how much *he* knows?"

"Oh God. I'll never be able to look him in the eye again."

"You? What about me? I'm the one banging his mother."

"Next time I see him give you a high-five…"

We sat there in the cold for several minutes, giggling like school kids who'd just heard a dirty joke.

When the giggles slowed, Grayson wrapped me in his arms, nuzzling my neck. "Speaking of the things in that drawer, want to head back inside? It really is freezing out here."

I gave in to the embrace and melted against him. "I'm supposed to be mad at you, you know."

He pulled his head up and stared at me. "For what?"

I wasn't sure myself. There just seemed to be a more defined line between our jobs with this case than others. The only thing different was Dr. Scranton. "I think Dr. Scranton's making too much of us working together."

"So you're supposed to be mad at *me*?"

It did sound ridiculous when he said it aloud. "I know our professional relationship is unconventional. It just seems like Felicia Scranton doesn't miss an opportunity to point that out. And you haven't been real quick to defend it."

"I've just tried to avoid it. You know, in some cities we'd be adversaries."

I didn't want to argue with him. I didn't want to be his enemy. I wanted to love him. And right now, I just wanted him. "Maybe that's why we're so good together. It's against the rules."

CHAPTER 17

The next morning, I called Aaron from the office and set up a lunch meeting at Minnie's Cafe for noon. I had doubts about working the project into an already tight schedule but wanted to hear him out. As expected, he jumped at the offer and rattled off a pre-production schedule before I shushed him. "We'll talk about all that at lunch." I said, wondering if I should already regret my decision to participate.

After hanging up, I pulled the yearbook from my bag. Turning to the senior pictures, I flipped to the page I had marked with a sticky note and scanned the page on the copier. When the image popped up on my computer, I zoomed in on Kelvin Dennis and printed the blown-up picture. I did the same with Kenny Dupree. Armed with the two copies, I told Nola to call if she needed me then headed back to Calvin Lee Andrews.

Bertie was home and welcomed me with a warm embrace, dish towel in hand. Soft around the edges, she defined sweetness and mothered Calvin like her main goal in life was to take care of her man. Standing in their living room, she looked over her shoulder toward the kitchen then spoke in a low voice. "Calvin told me why you came by the other day. Didn't offer much help, did he?"

I matched my tone to hers. "He suddenly lost his memory and even pretended to not remember Tommy was dead. I was concerned enough to talk to Doretha about it."

She put an arthritic-swollen hand to her mouth to suppress a giggle. "That rascal."

"You think he'll talk today?"

"I'll see if I can't coax it out of him. He's in the kitchen working on the toaster. One of the coils got bent and tears his toast up. Can't have his toast tearing up."

I followed Bertie into the kitchen. Calvin was at the oak table with the offending toaster and a cache of small tools in front of him. He glanced up from his work and smiled. "Come back, I see."

"I did. I just have a few more questions if you don't mind."

He dug deeper into the toaster and blew a heavy sigh. "I told you what I know and it weren't much."

I wasn't going to be deterred this time. You can lead me down the rabbit hole once, but seldom twice. "You also pretended to not know Tommy was dead. Cop killed in the line of duty. Everyone knew it."

"Killed in the line of duty. I hate to hear that."

Bertie spun around from her dishwashing, soap bubbles clinging to her hands. "Calvin Lee Andrews. What in the world is wrong with you? We went to that boy's funeral. Now you quit playing games with Ava and tell her what she needs to know."

He went back to his toaster. "'Needs to know' and 'wants to know' are two different things."

"Doretha told me why you might be reluctant to talk about that day at the mill. I get it, Calvin. You don't have to be afraid of coming forward."

"I've already told you all I know."

I pulled the two pictures out of my bag, unfolded them and slid them across the table. "Do you recognize either one of these two boys?"

He stared at the pictures longer than someone would if they didn't recognize them. The hesitation suggested memories were surfacing, whether he'd admit it or not.

"Calvin—were either of these boys at the mill that day?"

After another long pause, he tapped one of the pictures with the tip of the pliers. "That one. He was there."

I put the picture of Kelvin, the wife-beater, back in my bag. If Calvin Lee was right, Kenny Dupree didn't die in Vietnam. He died at the old mill. "Can you tell me what happened?"

Bertie abandoned the dishes and joined us at the table. She wiped her hands on the well-bleached dishtowel then reached out and patted her husband's hand. "It's okay, Baby. Ain't nothing to be scared of no more."

His body posture jostled with a bit of ruffled pride. "Wasn't scared. Just didn't want no trouble."

I offered a gentle smile. A slight gesture of my appreciation for asking him to revisit a time he'd obviously rather forget. "Do you remember what you saw, Calvin?"

He stared at the picture. "Used to be I'd see what I saw again every day in my head. Then one day, I went to bed that night telling myself I didn't see nothing that day. And I was happy 'bout that. Then the days stretched into weeks, then months and finally years. Never thought about it again until they closed the mill. All the secrets that ol' place had would die with it I reckoned."

There was only one secret I was interested in at that moment. "Can you tell me what you saw?"

He looked up from the toaster, eyes clouded with age, staring at me. "If I tell you, I don't want nothin' coming back on me. Understand?"

I wasn't going to argue or question him when I was this close. I nodded.

He motioned toward the picture. "That boy was talking to another man down near the woods. The guy here, in the picture, turned to leave and the other man pulled out a gun and shot him, I think."

"You're not sure?"

"The young guy turned to leave and then the other man pulled something out of his pocket. Next thing I knew the young guy dropped like a lead balloon." He slammed his hand against the table.

I flinched at the *pop* of his hand. "Did you hear a gunshot?"

Calvin slowly shook his head. "No, but I was at the back door of the dying room. Lot of noise going on."

"Did you recognize the other guy?"

"I'd seen him around. I think he worked the night shift 'cause I'd pass him coming and going some."

"You didn't know his name?"

"I kept to myself, Miss Ava. Didn't want no trouble from anyone."

Exactly what Doretha had said. There was safety in silence. "Can you describe him?"

Calvin shrugged, crinkled his face up like it would help him remember. "Wasn't nothing that stood out on him if that's what you mean. Just your average guy.

"Were they about the same age?"

"Hard to tell from a distance. I remember seeing him 'round the mill, round town some and he looked to be maybe in his twenties."

My breath hitched. "You saw him around town?"

"Saw him once or twice at the hardware store. He always had that boy with him."

I leaned into the table, my interest now in overdrive. "What boy?"

"That one ain't right in the head."

My chest tightened. "Keeper McCarter?"

"Is that what they call him? Never knew his name."

Bertie chimed in. "The curly-haired fella that sweeps floors at the fire department sometimes? Is that him?"

That was Keeper alright. "Calvin—what year was this? Do you remember?"

"What year was the killing or what year'd I see him at the hardware store?"

"Both."

He tapped a long, yellowed fingernail on the wooden table in a steady rhythm. After giving the question some thought, he finally answered. "Can't say for sure but it seems like it would be around 1969, '70, maybe. I'd stepped outside to smoke when I saw it and I gave up the cigarettes in '70."

"And this was on the back side of the building?"

"Yessir. Didn't like going out on the side of the building where the others went. Too much trouble lurking around." His eyes reflected a memory he wasn't comfortable with.

I wondered if it was really trouble Calvin had hoped to avoid or if it was that a black man wasn't invited to share a smoke break with "the good ol' boys?" Hard to fathom a time like that even existed. Despite the problem with the segregated break area, a murder took place on the opposite side of the building.

Was the killer a "good ol' boy?" How'd he know Kenny? If it happened in '69, Kenny would have just been discharged. "Do you remember what month it was?"

"Had to have been summer because the trees were full. And I remember it being hot as blazes."

"So June, July maybe?"

"Have to be June. Mill always shut down the month of July."

I could see the beginnings of a timeline developing. Kenny Dupree's parents went to the newspaper in June 1969 to say their son didn't come home, Calvin witnessed someone we believe to be Kenny, murdered the same month. But why would Kenny not tell anyone he was back? If he did, it was the wrong person.

The second part of the equation was Keeper. "When did you see the same man at the hardware store?"

"Don't remember 'xactly."

"How old was the boy that was with him?"

"Well, he weren't a *boy*, I don't think. He was grown, tall as the other man."

Bertie added, "You know how with the simple-minded ones we always think of them as children even after they're adults. No matter how tall they are."

I thought of Keeper watching that game show. I heard him cackling and clapping his hands. The excitement that filled him whenever he greeted me. So child-like. "Had this been recently that you saw them together?"

Calvin shrugged. "Maybe two, three years ago."

I'm not sure what bothered me more. A cold-blooded murderer walking around Jackson Creek or the fact Keeper was with him.

CHAPTER 18

Sitting in Minnie's Cafe waiting on Aaron, I stared at every man that came through the door, wondering if he could be the one who Calvin Lee saw kill Kenny Dupree. I knew most of them and counted most out immediately. Good people. The kind that helps a neighbor, not kills them. Frank Stiller pitched in and baled hay for Ned Barrett's horses when Ned was sick from chemo. Wylie Cline timbered over two acres of his property and bundled the wood, giving it away in cords to single moms and the elderly. Even delivered it.

These were people who lived right. They weren't murderers. Maybe Kenny's death was an act of rage? Jails were filled with people who lashed out in a fit of rage. But if they had done it once, what would keep them from doing it again?

Although my own mother swore she'd killed my father in a fit of rage, it was more out of self-preservation than a confession. Maybe if the prosecutor felt sorry for her, they'd impose a lighter sentence. After all those years of abuse, she claimed she just snapped. Something had snapped but it was days before she blew him all to hell with a shotgun. I watched her load the gun two days before she shot him. She put a finger to her lips to warn me not to tell. My mother—my security—had made me her accomplice. I never did tell, kept her secret all these years, but in the court's eyes they saw it as premeditated despite the rage.

Was Keeper the common link between the victim and the killer? If the victim was, in fact, Kenny Dupree, then there was definitely a connection to Keeper. The tie that bound it all together was Mary.

I began to second-guess myself for scheduling this meeting with Aaron. There was a lot going on right now that involved Mary. She may not want to participate in the making of a documentary, to share her gifts with an audience. The possibility her high school sweetheart died right here rather than lingering in the jungles of a foreign country was real. That was a lot for anyone to take in. Did she know the man who killed him? The man who took her baby's father away from her? Chances are she did if the man was with Keeper at the hardware store. Mary hovered over Keeper like he was still a toddler. It was just human instinct to treat someone like Keeper as if they were a child. I did. Knowing Keeper was with this man gave me goosebumps on my arms, made my insides boil with anger. In that respect, I understood rage. Aaron came in and waved as if I wouldn't recognize him. He wasn't alone. A guy around the same age came in with him and followed Aaron back to my booth. He was handsome like Aaron, a little more rugged, bulkier in his fisherman knit sweater and Columbia down jacket.

Aaron slid into the booth opposite me. The other guy offered his hand first. "Blayne Bell, videographer."

Bell? I wagged a finger between the two. "Are y'all—"

"Brothers," Aaron offered.

Blayne joined his brother in the booth. "And partners."

I looked at Aaron. "Oh. I wasn't aware there was a partner."

He started to speak but his brother jumped in. "Has Aaron been keeping me a secret again? You know, he locked me in a room once, but I escaped."

Aaron rolled his eyes, jokingly. "Pardon my brother. Unfortunately, he does come with the deal."

Blayne cocked his head toward Aaron. "He's the money, I'm the talent."

Diane dropped menus off at our booth and took our drink order before hurrying on to the next table. She yelled at the girl at the register to not forget the man's to-go order in the kitchen.

"So, I watched *Easter's Promise* last night. I have to say I was impressed."

A smile spread across Aaron's face. "Thanks. I am rather proud of that one."

"It was shortlisted for an Academy Award," Blayne added, just as proud.

I knew it was a quality film but didn't realize it had been considered for awards. "You need to add that to your business card," I scolded Aaron for his modesty.

Aaron blushed. "Well, I can't take all the credit for that. The cinematography in that one was simply gorgeous."

Blayne grinned, cleared his throat. "And who was the head of cinematography?"

I forced a laugh and was sure it sounded fake. Nothing personal against either of them. I just couldn't move away from the investigation. Thoughts of Mary and Keeper wouldn't go away no matter how hard I tried to push them out of my head.

Focus. Be in the moment. Participate. Fortunately, Diane brought our drinks right then and saved me from having to apologize for my scattered thoughts.

She handed out paper-wrapped straws with the drinks. "Y'all ready to order?"

"I am," I said then realized how quickly I'd answered.

Diane laughed. "Hungry?"

"Starving. What's the soup of the day?"

"Tater. Made it myself."

The joys of owning a small business. You do it all. I could relate. "I'll have a bowl of that. With bacon crumbles, right?"

"You got it. Gentleman, y'all decided yet?"

Aaron looked at me. "I guess the potato soup is good?"

"Best around." And it was. Thick and creamy, really just a half-cup of cream shy of being mashed potatoes with chives, onions and cheese. And bacon crumbles on request.

Both Aaron and Blayne ordered the soup. Diane yelled out the order then trotted over to the register to help the cashier with a credit card payment. Not that mountain people weren't used to credit cards, we just preferred cash.

"So," Aaron said, "I thought we'd start shooting some exterior footage as soon as possible—"

Blayne jumped in. "With snow on the ground, dead trees, real bleak looking. You know...depressing, like one of the misconceptions about the area."

I jerked my hand up to stop him right there. "No. Absolutely not."

Surprise registered on both their faces. They stared at me, then one another, then back to me.

I pointed a stern finger at Aaron. "You said no clichés. You promised, Aaron. I'll walk away from this project right now if that's the way you're going with it."

Aaron raised both hands, defending his honor, and his

vision. Had he lied to me about the vision? "Just hear us out, okay?" he said.

I shoved my back against the booth, the cracked vinyl poking through my sweater. Arms folded as tight as my lips were drawn.

Aaron proceeded cautiously with a voice teetering on tentative. "In order to show the good, in the end—because that's what we want to end on, the good—we have to start with the bad. The snow, the bleakness...the depression. All of that *is* a misconception. So we begin it with some footage of winter, and end it with spring."

"It's a symbolic transition," Blayne said. "There's light at the end of the tunnel type thing. New life."

After I calmed down, I understood. It was all about transition. Symbolic, or not. It still made me nervous. Maybe it was knowing a murderer was walking amongst us that made me apprehensive about showing *any* of the bad. Murderers right in there with the moonshiners and the dirt poor.

"Ava, I promise. No clichés. Just the truth."

Maybe it was the truth I was afraid of? What if the truth was a cliché? Warts and blemishes and bad people. Long buried secrets and buried bodies. What if *that's* who we were? Who we truly were.

Blayne took his phone out and punched around on the screen, then turned it toward me. "What do you see?"

A peach-colored rose, wet from morning dew or perhaps a gentle rain. The definition of each water drop was breathtaking. "A rose."

"Pretty isn't it?"

Of course it was pretty. It was beautiful. Who couldn't see that? "It's very pretty."

"You see the thorns?"

The question threw me. I blinked at Blayne then stared at the picture again. *There*. There they were. One, two. Three skin-piercing thorns.

"They weren't the first thing you noticed were they? They were overshadowed by the sheer beauty of the rose."

It was all I could do to not cry. Damn, if he wasn't right. There would always be ugly. The gut-stabbing awful bad-to-the-bone ugly. The meth-heads and opioid freaks and their self-inflicted poverty, the toothless, uneducated dimwits who didn't have an excuse like Keeper did. They were the thorns amongst the roses.

I slowly nodded, finally understanding. It was impossible to have one without the other. "I get it," I said, my voice slight but sure.

Diane returned to the booth with our soups. After setting each one down, she dug in the pocket of her apron then tossed several packs of saltines on the table. "Anything else?"

"Do you have any croutons?" Blayne said.

Diane's brows reacted individually, one going up, one arching down. "Croutons?"

"Yeah—you know, like salad croutons."

"I know what croutons are. Just ain't never heard putting 'em in soup. I'll bring you some in a minute." She headed back to the kitchen, shaking her head and mumbling about "damn yankees."

I felt the need to apologize for Diane's rudeness but the words wouldn't come. Diane was Diane. Thorns and all. I gnawed on my bottom lip instead.

"Are we good with getting some winter shots?" Aaron said.

I gave him my blessing then dove into the soup. What

Diane lacked in manners she more than made up for with her talent in the kitchen.

Blayne waved his spoon around between bites, not waiting on the croutons. "I'd actually like some shots of an area where the snow might still cover the ground. Any ideas?"

"There are several ski resorts around here, right?" Aaron said.

I waved them both off. "There are but I don't think you'd get the look you're hoping for. They're not *bleak* at all."

Aaron gazed at the bowl of soup like it was a secret treasure. Maybe it was. At least to visitors. "This is really good. What about shooting up around the granny witch's place? That was pretty secluded. What was her name?"

"Mary," I whispered. "I don't want to involve her just yet."

If at all. There were other granny women throughout this part of Appalachia, but I didn't know them like I knew Mary. There were trust issues with people in these hills and hollers. A trustworthy relationship took years to cultivate. The distrust, however, was passed down from generation to generation.

"Know of anywhere else?" Aaron said.

The river behind my house would be perfect. Snow still covered the shaded bank. The surrounding trees were leaf-less. "My backyard."

Aaron's mouth formed a perfect "O." "Yes! Perfect."

My mood took a nose dive and the anger nearly rehashed. I glared at him, the frown on my face unmistakable.

"I mean...what I saw of it," Aaron said, quickly backtracking.

"Which you won't see again unless you're what?"

"Invited."

I finished my soup, my hunger satiated. My nerves were

still on edge, goosebumps still sprouting on my arms, and Keeper and Mary still on my mind.

CHAPTER 19

I left Aaron and Blayne at the diner devising a production schedule. My insides were on fire with knowledge I couldn't share with them. I *wouldn't* share with them. Even telling Grayson presented problems. A thin line existed between the man I shared my bed with and the sheriff of Jackson County. The boundary moved fluidly but it was always there. Still, I had to tell him what Calvin saw. There was no way I could hold it back from him. Fingers crossed he'd let *me* tell Mary when the time was right.

His Expedition was in the parking lot at the sheriff's department. I sat in the Tahoe staring at the front door, the heater's air blowing hot against my face. I hoped Dr. Scranton wasn't with him. My mind wasn't prepared to deal with her today.

I turned the car off, sat there for another minute to gather my nerve, then went inside. Gave Annie a long hug. Maybe killing time to avoid the inevitable? I had to tell him—there was just no way around it. Withholding information as potent as someone witnessing a murder was a deal breaker. Professionally, and personally.

After the embrace, Annie said, "He's in his office. Alone. Thank God."

A tiny smile crept across my lips. "You mean Dr. Scranton?"

"Those brainy kinds have no common sense or social manners if you ask me."

Didn't matter if someone asked her or not, Annie was going to voice her opinion.

What inappropriate comment had the redhead made this time? I couldn't help but wonder what Dr. Scranton had done to offend Annie. Someone who'd heard it all, seen it all. If I weren't in such a jam over telling Grayson, I might have giggled. As it were, I stood there working a tiny smile so I wouldn't look like a total bitch.

Before I headed to his office, Grayson came out with a stack of papers to be filed. He handed them off to Annie. Life went on despite the death of Kenny Dupree.

"Got a minute?" I asked.

He studied me for a second, the concern in his Sinatra-blue eyes proof he knew me well. "Sure. Come on back."

I followed him to his office where he closed the door behind us. The butterflies in my stomach had morphed into stomping elephants. Grayson moved around behind his desk, watching me with his cop's eyes. The man could see right through me. He knew every heartbeat, the way it sounded, their rhythm against my chest.

"We have a problem." I rubbed my hands on my jeans, transferring the moisture to the denim.

I didn't want to sit. My legs would bounce too much. I didn't want to pace. That would bring on jumbled thoughts. So I stood there, in front of his desk, like a terrified school kid addressing the principal.

I steadied my breath then spit out the words like they were flaming embers. "Calvin Lee Andrews witnessed the murder."

He didn't say anything at first. Just stared at me. He then motioned for me to sit. "You spoke to him again?"

Nodding, I sat in the guest chair, consciously willing my legs to still. "I went by there this morning. I took the yearbook and showed him the picture of Kenny Dupree. He ID'd him as the victim."

Grayson eased back in his chair and scratched at the day-old stubble lining his chin. "You think it could have been the power of suggestion?"

I blinked at the question, shook off the sting. Hands clasped together. To keep them from shaking, and to keep from choking him. "I showed him other pictures." The words were plain enough, the tone biting.

"Calm down. I didn't mean it like that." His own tone softened, knowing he needed to tread carefully. "Tell me what he said."

I put aside the bruised feelings for the sake of Mary and Keeper, telling him everything Calvin had shared with me. Even why Calvin had never come forward.

"And he's sure the man worked at the mill?"

"Yes. He just didn't know his name. He didn't socialize with coworkers."

"Could he give you a date?"

I shook my head. "Not an exact but we did narrow it down. He remembered it was hot and the trees were full. The mill always shut down in July, and Dupree's parents went to the paper in June of 1969 saying he never came home."

"Did he say how old the shooter was?"

"Maybe in his twenties." I did the math in my head to figure a current age. "If he's still alive, he'd probably be in his seventies now."

"When's the last time Calvin saw him?"

"Two or three years ago. He saw him at the hardware store—with Keeper." I nearly choked on the name. Everything in me fought against the thought of Keeper with that man. Keeper trusted wholly, with his entire being. He didn't know any other way.

"Does Mary know?"

My heart sank as I considered that question. "She has to know the man. She's not going to let Keeper go off with someone she doesn't know. She guards him like a momma bear. You know that."

As long as I could remember, Mary was almost too protective of her boy. Despite his diminished mental abilities, Keeper was a grown man, with the strength of two. Did his innocence come naturally from not understanding the world around him, or from being sheltered from that world? Mary lived in fear someone would take her baby away from her, she'd told me that. She'd never told Kenny's parents about their grandson out of that fear. What would she have done if Kenny had been the one to try and take him away?

That thought scared me. There was no way Mary could have been involved in what happened. The pain of *not knowing* was too real.

"Mary would never...she would never be a part of hurting someone like that." My voice quivered with emotion. How far does a mother go to protect her child?

One shell? Two shells? How many did my mother load? Her eyes dark, empty. She's looking at me now. Finger to her lips. Everything's gonna be alright, she'd whisper to me later that night. Don't worry about a thing. Momma's gonna take care of it. The blast. The blood. My daddy, dead. My ears! Oh my ears! Momma, my ears! I can't hear you. The tears are stinging my eyes. They're burning. Am I crying because of the ringing in my ears, or for my daddy? Momma, hold me. Make it go away.

My lungs grasped for air. I pushed up out the chair as thoughts surfaced through my head like the muzzle flash from her shotgun. My chest cramped with tightness. "Oh my God, Grayson. What if she was—"

He rushed around the desk, reaching for me. "You're overthinking. There's no proof Mary was involved."

"But what if she was?"

"We'll deal with it. Right now, we need to positively ID the remains." Ever the voice of reason.

I knew that. I just couldn't move passed the thought that Mary may know the man who killed Keeper's father. It didn't make her involved in the murder. Knowing the murderer didn't make her an accomplice. It would just make the final outcome hurt all the more.

Grayson wrapped his arms around me, smoothing my hair like I was an upset child. Maybe I was. Impatient and impulsive, I had to rein myself in. This wasn't about me. I moved away from him and went over to the window. Dust was an inch thick on the blinds, adding to the bleakness of winter through the window.

"Ava—even if we got a DNA sample from Keeper, and it did match the remains, all that proves is that they're related. It doesn't prove it's Kenny Dupree."

I heard him talking, even listened, but the words melded together like the dingy world outside the window. A few days ago, it was pristine and white. Crystal clear and sharp. Like walking in the woods on a snowy day where the sound carried, amplified in its clarity. I could hear Pudge Collins' beagles baying again. Tucker, lost from the pack, digging up a past that would either implicate a good friend, or bring her relief. Or heartache.

"Let Dr. Scranton do her job. We'll have enough to work with soon."

I spun around not wanting to bank Mary and Keeper's future on Dr. Scranton's timeframe. It was a cold case, no doubt. It was probably an isolated incident where there was an intended target and no one else was ever in danger.

Except perhaps Keeper. "I can't accept that, Grayson. I can't sit by and wait. I brought a horrible pain on Mary by showing her that picture. The least I can do is bring her resolution."

He sighed heavily and leaned on his desk. "Even if it means hurting her even more? She's moved on. Maybe she doesn't want to know the truth. Have you thought of that? You said she refused to acknowledge the picture could have been Dupree."

Was there really anything worse than not knowing? "She didn't want to admit it because she couldn't accept the fact he'd come back and didn't tell her."

"So you're going to prove her wrong?"

I flinched, batting back the truth. "It's not about proving her wrong—it's about giving her an answer."

"Whether she wants it or not?"

A twinge of burning anger bubbled in my gut. I needed to get out of there before it turned to red-orange lava and spewed out in words I'd regret. "Okay," I muttered, sucking in a deep breath. Hands up to signify a truce, or maybe to tell him to back off. "You do your job and I'll do mine."

"You're not going to let it go, are you?"

"A man was murdered, Grayson. There's still a bullet in his skull. Are *you* going to let that go?"

He ran his tongue around the inside of his mouth, poking around his cheeks. I'd hit a nerve and I didn't regret it. He moved back behind his desk and sat down, rolled his chair up and shuffled through a small stack of file folders. Apparently this meeting was over. The desk phone trilled, startling us both. He punched the speaker button. "What is it, Annie?"

The voice warbled through the speaker, sounding much more distant than the next room. "I have Dr. Scranton for you."

Grayson and I exchanged glances but he made no effort to take the call privately. "Put her through." Annie grumbled something then transferred the call. "Hey, Felicia. What's up?"

Felicia? They were on a first name basis? I breathed deeply. This wasn't about me.

"I recovered the bullet. If you can find the gun, you should be able to match it."

The cold case had just heated up.

CHAPTER 20

I left Grayson's office more determined than ever to find an answer for Mary. The scientific aspects of finding skeletal remains shouldn't overshadow the human part of the equation. Mary deserved to know what happened to her high school sweetheart and the father of her baby. Kenny Dupree's family deserved to know he hadn't discarded ties and that he had come home. And Keeper needed to know there were people he shouldn't hang around with.

That bugged me more than anything. I'd never questioned Mary on what Keeper knew about his father, just assumed he wouldn't understand if she told him. Had he ever questioned her on it? Did he wonder about it? I knew he was close to his grandfather. Did he even understand family relationships?

I was often angry that my own parents denied my kids the bond between grandparents and children. Tommy's father was dead, but his mother did keep in contact with Cole and Emma. At least they had that. No uncles, no aunts. Not even a cousin. All we had was each other and Doretha. All Keeper had was Mary and an uncle.

Back at the office, life went on with the normal buzz of

publication day. Nola fielding calls about why the recipe was omitted and Quinn dodging bullets from zoning board members. Danny, the layout man, already at work designing new ads.

As I sat down at my desk, Nola spun her chair around to face me. "Four calls so far about the human remains. Three of them have family missing and one wants to know if we're all in danger."

Three people in Jackson Creek with family missing? "Can I see those names?"

Nola rolled her chair over and handed the list to me. "One of them—Kristy Marsh—thinks it's her husband."

I stared at the names. "Ricky Marsh? He ran off with their kids' Sunday School teacher."

Nola nodded. "Yep. I didn't want to point that out to her. What do you want me to do if any others call?"

I put the list on my desk then powered up my computer. "Tell them they need to call the sheriff's department rather than us."

Like Grayson wasn't pissed enough with me. Now he was going to start getting calls left and right on missing loved ones. Why weren't these people reported missing in the first place? I glared at the names again, recognizing two of the three. I didn't count Ricky Marsh.

Kirby Danforth called in about his wife. Poor thing died of cancer last year. Kirby couldn't accept she was gone even though he buried her in the Methodist church cemetery. I made a mental note to check on him. Married fifty-plus years. I covered their fiftieth anniversary, whenever it was. A couple years ago at least. They had three kids and I wondered where they were? Were they checking in on their daddy?

I pushed my hands through my hair, the tiredness catching up with me. Pushed thoughts of Kirby Danforth, needy and lonely, aside. I couldn't save the world and had never hoped to. Back and forth like a rocking boat on what I could do, should do, and wanted to do. Sometimes the boat was in the middle of a storm, like now. Other times, a gentle rocking one way or the other brought clarity.

I jotted it on my calendar—check on Kirby. The whole world was out of reach, but my little corner might be doable. After I found out what happened to Kenny Dupree.

I dug through public records for the Dupree siblings until I came up with two names. Russell Dupree and Belinda Whitmore. Both lived in Knoxville. Russell didn't answer the phone. Belinda did, sounding easy going and pleasant. I introduced myself.

"You're with a newspaper?" She said between another conversation. "Momma, don't you want your peaches?"

"Yes, I'm with the *Jackson Creek Chronicle*. I believe y'all used to live in Jackson Creek."

"Oh, yeah. Yeah, we did. Would you rather have some pears? Do you mind holding just a minute? Let me get Momma settled."

Katherine Dupree had to be in her nineties or close to it. A nursing home, maybe? "Go ahead. I don't mind holding."

Chatter filtered through the phone with bits and pieces of conversations between several people. Someone banging a light, happy tune on a piano in the background. After a minute or two, Belinda came back on the line and the other noises fell silent as a door closed. "I'm so sorry about that. It's afternoon fellowship time at the nursing home and it gets a little crazy. Now how can I help you?" Her voice was still light and playful. I hoped she'd remain this cheerful.

"I'd like to visit with you about your brother, Kenny." There. I'd said it. I held my breath waiting for her reaction.

Minutes of silence ticked off in my mind like a metronome until she finally responded. "I'm sorry, but my brother Kenny died in Vietnam."

"I'd heard that and I'm very sorry. I'm writing an article about local veterans and Kenny's name came up. I'd like to include him in the story." I hadn't lied. Every word of that was the truth.

"Well, I guess that would be alright. Momma has a scrapbook of newspaper articles about Kenny. She has some letters from the army and stuff."

Was Katherine still in her right mind? Could she remember that far back?

Knoxville was a three-hour drive and it was too late to head out now. I didn't want to feed the kids pizza or cereal again. They needed a meal so I would feel less guilty about one thing. "Do you think you could make time to see me tomorrow?"

"I suppose that would be fine. Do you know what time?"

I calculated the time to get the kids up and to school, Ivy to Doretha's, and then hit the road. "How about eleven?"

"I'm usually at the nursing home by then but I guess I could come a little later."

"Oh no—I wouldn't want you to do that. Why don't I meet you there at the nursing home? Maybe your mother would like to show me her scrapbooks?"

Belinda cackled. "Oh my gosh, she'll talk your ear off."

"Is she still mentally sharp?"

"As a tack. Watches *Jeopardy* every night and most of the time gets the final question."

That's what I wanted to hear. "That's good. I can't wait to meet her."

I wondered if she'd remember Mary? Did she even know she had a grandson? It wasn't my place to tell her. I couldn't do that to Mary. Not that the fear of someone taking her son away still existed, especially that Keeper was a grown man, but sharing that news with the Dupree family would be her decision. Not mine.

Belinda gave me the address of the nursing home. "When you come in just tell them at the front desk you're there to see me. They'll come get me."

I gave her my number in case something came up and she wouldn't be there. "I'm looking forward to meeting you tomorrow."

After we hung up, I finally looked over the paper. Front page, above the fold was a picture of the tented crime scene. The article was bare-bones, no frills or fluff. A couple quotes from Grayson, even a few from Dr. Scranton. In the end it left more questions than answers.

Hopefully the next issue would answer them.

I left the office and swung by Doretha's to pick up Ivy. I loved seeing the toddler and it warmed my heart when she wrapped her dimpled arms around my neck, smothering me with her wet kisses.

Doretha stood at the stove stirring an industrial sized pot of spaghetti sauce. Sweat glistened against her skin from the heat accumulating in the small kitchen. Moisture clung to the windows. "I heard you saw Calvin Lee."

Slow to answer, I lowered Ivy to the ground and showed her a few toys. "I had to, Doretha. You knew that."

She gave me a side-eye glare. "Yep, I knew it alright. That's why I called and warned him."

With her since I was eight years-old, she knew me so well.

"He witnessed a murder."

She stopped stirring but didn't turn around to look at me, the wooden spoon hovering just above the sauce. "He told you that?"

"Yes. I didn't have to pry it out of him either." I said it with a touch of snideness like it was something to be proud of.

Doretha lowered the spoon into the sauce and resumed her stirring, slower than before. "I'm glad you got what you wanted."

Her attitude pricked me hard square in the chest. "Doretha, he witnessed a murder. He saw a co-worker kill another man."

"And he is going to have to testify to that? Is he going to get dragged into court as an eyewitness?"

She slapped the spoon against the side of the pot then dropped it on a paper towel spread on the counter.

I stumbled over an answer, reaching for reassuring words. "Hopefully, there'll be enough physical evidence they won't need an eyewitness. Besides...you know how it is with eyewitness testimonies. They say they're the least reliable."

The words were true, but I was rambling, hoping to smooth ruffled feathers. And Doretha saw right through them. She turned around and faced me, exhaling through her nose. "Then why'd you push him?"

"He offered a starting point. He gave me something to work with. Calvin Lee did a good thing, Doretha."

"Fifty years after the fact. You don't think people aren't going to question why he never came forward before now?"

Maybe I was stubborn beyond reason, hard-headed to the point of frustration, but I didn't get the bigger issue. Calvin was scared to come forward. We knew that. It was a fact. A black man in that day and age did better to pretend he didn't see anything. I *had* learned that during this whole thing. But now, there seemed to be something else lurking beneath the surface.

Doretha turned the sauce down then slowly moved to the little dinette table. She grimaced, lowering herself onto one of the chairs, and I saw the pain in her eyes. She hid the arthritis behind laughs and long pants. After waving a hand for me to join her, a look of resignation shadowed her face that I'd never seen before. In all the years I'd known her, she was the strong one. The one who held the world together when it was falling apart, offered words of comfort from the good book or her own wisdom. "There's more to the story," she said in a slight voice.

CHAPTER 21

I'd only seen Doretha tear up a few times in my life and most of those involved lifting her arms to heaven and shouting a praise. But she was teary-eyed now. And much quieter than her usual self. Whatever secrets she and Calvin were holding onto were buried deep and painful to revisit. I braced myself for the damage I'd done by enlisting Calvin's help.

She dabbed a tissue at her cheek then tucked it into the top of her bra. Like she'd done so many times before. This time was different. They weren't joy-filled tears brought on by the Holy Spirit. "My kin folk ain't from 'round here. We came from Chicago."

Chicago? I couldn't wrap my head around that. Maybe because I grew up in this house, I assumed Doretha had never lived anywhere other than right here where we sat. The few times I asked about her family, she'd said we were her family. Us—all the foster kids—and Calvin Lee. She'd laugh it off and say family wasn't always blood related. That theme was becoming too familiar.

I didn't say anything, choosing to let her talk. "Calvin and I were born in The Windy City and lived there for a good while.

Calvin, at least until he was a teenager. He found his way here to Jackson Creek and met Bertie. Settled down."

Her hands shook and she covered one with the other to quiet the nerves. She looked so much older than I remembered. She'd aged twenty years in the last half hour. Whatever I'd done to bring this on, I'd never forgive myself.

I reached out and squeezed her hand. "Doretha...you don't have to tell me."

"Calvin can't testify, Baby Doll. He's a wanted man."

My ribs tightened and clutched the breath right out of my lungs. I gasped for needed air as my heart pounded in my chest. "Oh, God—Doretha. I didn't know," I stuttered and stumbled all over the words. *What had I done?*

She shook her head back and forth. Her braids clacked a spastic rhythm. "No one knows."

I swallowed a deluge of threatening tears, refusing to cry. I'd screwed this up and balling like a baby wasn't going to fix it. "We'll figure a way out. Grayson has the bullet. If we can find the gun, we won't even need Calvin's testimony."

Deep in my heart I knew the only thing the bullet and the gun would prove was the cause of death. The only way to prove *who* was by luck or a witness. As the only witness, Calvin's luck might have just run out.

It was no wonder he didn't want to get involved. Yet I dragged him into it kicking and screaming. "What did he do?"

Eyes cast downward, she stared at her hands, knuckles swollen with age. "He was in the wrong place at the wrong time. Did something stupid."

I urged her to go on. I wanted to hear the story, hear the truth.

"He and some friends got brave one night and mouthed off

to a police officer. They were loitering 'round a liquor store and the policeman thought they were gonna try and rob it. They was just hanging out like teenagers'll do. Weren't causing no trouble." She teared up again and reached for her tissue.

After wiping her eyes she continued, "One of the boys mouthed off to the officer and the cop hit him with his billy stick. Busted his head wide open. Calvin weren't no troublemaker, but he stood up against what he thought was wrong. He punched the cop and made him fall. Banged his head all up on the curb. Said Calvin tried to kill him. Next thing we know, they saying all around Calvin was gonna be charged with attempted murder and assault on a police officer. Had no choice but to run. Been on the run ever since." She took a breath and finally looked up.

"But why didn't he just tell the truth? He had witnesses to back him up, right?"

Doretha made a poor attempt at a chuckle. "Ava...this was the early sixties, Baby Doll. Black boy takes a swing at a white cop? Besides, all the other witnesses were black boys, too."

"But that was over fifty years ago. There has to be a statute of limitations."

"Not on the attempted murder of a police officer. At least there wasn't back then."

She sniffled then dabbed at her eyes again with finality. Pushing up from the chair, she wobbled painfully to the stove. Age had crept up on her in the last hour. She tended to the spaghetti sauce, dipping a ladle full into a small bowl. The bowl was ivory-colored with a chip around the edge, stained pale orange from years of being the tasting vessel. I was maybe ten and with her when she bought it for a dime at a yard sale. Funny, the things you remember from childhood.

Doretha popped a spoon in the taste bowl then brought it over to the table. She slid it in front of me. "I know it's your favorite."

As much as I wanted to devour the sauce, I let it cool a moment, hoping to continue the conversation while *it* was still hot. There was so much buried beneath the surface and we were treading water. "Does Bertie know?"

"Not to my knowledge. Calvin didn't want *anyone* to know. He was ashamed, and scared."

They'd been married all these years and she didn't know? How do you keep a secret that big for that long? Images rolled through my mind like a movie of Bertie rolling her eyes at him while he worked on the toaster, the grin that followed. The pride that flowed through them when talking about their kids and grandkids, the pride in one another. This secret Calvin Lee had carried for so long—would Bertie, his Bertie, accept it when it came out? When it came out because of something I'd pressured her husband into doing.

My part in all this sat like an elephant on my shoulders. No matter which way I turned to escape the burden of knowing I was the cause, the elephant wobbled but hung on. If I'd caused this mess, I wanted to know everything about it. "Did you follow Calvin to Jackson Creek?"

She nodded. "Poppa was already dead before Calvin left and it was just me and Momma. When she caught pneumonia and died, wasn't no use in me hanging around Chicago. I stayed about a year, but...just wasn't the same." A heavy frown tugged the corners of her mouth downward, emphasizing the lines feathering outward from her cracked lips. "Besides, I needed to tell Calvin 'bout Momma. No one should have to go through life not knowing their Momma's dead."

Or their son's father.

I took a tiny bite of the sauce although my insides were on fire. My stomach churned from stress. If anything happened to Calvin because of this, I wouldn't be able to live with myself. And I'd told Grayson everything Calvin Lee had told me. About actually witnessing the murder. How in the world could I retract what I'd said? I couldn't pretend I'd never said it. Grayson would see right through it and that would make him all the more determined to dig deeper.

There was still one piece that didn't fit the puzzle. Why'd Calvin tell me what he saw? "Doretha, why didn't Calvin just keep pretending he didn't know anything? When he started talking about Tommy, he had me convinced he was suffering from dementia."

Her frown slowly morphed into a smile. A slight one, but a smile all the same. "He knew you'd keep digging. And...he didn't want to be the cause of a lie between me and you."

It was a noble thought, but he was living a lie, and the truth was Doretha *was* involved. I wasn't going to question it with her. I'd done enough damage. Whether I agreed with it or not, there was a difference between lying and withholding the truth. And with this new knowledge, that's exactly what I would be doing, too.

CHAPTER 22

Golden Hearts Nursing Center sat on the outskirts of Knoxville, tucked into a valley surrounded by the Smoky Mountains. A single-level brick building with a green metal roof looked welcoming despite it being the end of the road for many. I wondered if that was the situation for Katherine Dupree.

I'd hit the road after dropping Ivy off and made good time, pulling into the parking lot at ten forty-five. Doretha had wrapped me in a tight hug when I handed over Ivy and told me not to worry—everything would work out. I usually believed her. This time I wasn't so sure.

Winter hung over the rolling peaks of the Smokies like a claw ready to bear down at any minute. I lingered in the Tahoe, enjoying the warmth before making a run for the double glass front doors. Coated my lips with ChapStick, pulled my wool toboggan on and down to my ears then sprinted to the covered entrance. I started to jerk the door open but nearly jerked my shoulder out of socket instead. Neither door budged but an intercom speaker mounted on the side wall crackled and buzzed.

"Can I help you?" A muffled voice asked.

I pushed the red button. "Ava Logan here to see Belinda

Whitmore. She's expecting me."

A stiff wind infiltrated the alcove and made my eyes water. I appreciated security, just not on days when it was twenty-six degrees with a windchill. After what seemed like an eternity, the double doors clicked open. The lobby was decorated in earthy tones of muted yellows and pale greens, soft leather furniture in muted brown, and original artwork in custom frames. A self-serve coffee bar was stationed under a picture window offering a view of the parking lot and beyond that, a majestic scene of the Smokies. Nothing about Golden Hearts Nursing Home reeked cheap. The only thing I knew about the Dupree's finances was what Mary had told me—they were well off. At least they had been back then. This type of home could drain a bank account.

A middle-aged receptionist smiled at me from behind a massive red oak desk on the far wall. Her name tag said, "Wendi."

"Belinda will be right up. Help yourself to a cup of coffee or hot chocolate while you wait. It's brutal out there."

If the rest of the center was as nice as the reception area, Katherine Dupree was in good hands. Two Keurig machines with three trees filled with a variety of flavors beat the crap out of hours-old industrial strength java. I fixed myself a cup of Southern Pecan.

A single door on the same wall as Wendi clicked open and a tall, slender woman came out. Belinda Whitmore, no doubt. The resemblance to not only her brother, but the nephew she knew nothing about was striking. The dark hooded eyes, wavy hair, and Keeper's smile. She wore dark jeans and a soft pink cashmere sweater, simple hoop earrings and a matching chain necklace. Very little makeup, but really, no need. Casual, but classic and well-maintained described her.

"Ava?"

"Yes." I transferred my coffee to my left hand so I could offer my right. She took it gladly, and I said, "I'm so glad you could meet me."

"Of course. I must say, I am rather curious about how my brother fits into the story."

Weren't we all.

Before I was allowed beyond the lobby, I had to sign in where Wendi indicated on the register. She gave me an orange Visitor badge I attached to my coat. It was only then she clicked the door open and gave me the okay to follow Belinda.

"I guess no one gets in that's not supposed to be here," I said.

"It's not so much as someone getting in as much as it is someone getting out that's not supposed to."

I could understand that. Someone wandering off in these mountains spelled disaster. The terrain was breathtakingly beautiful but posed threats from the weather, bears and falls.

The deeper we walked into the building the more I became aware of the smell. It wasn't the medicinal smell of ammonia or menthol rub, or even the unpleasant bodily function odors that often permeated hospitals and nursing homes. These halls smelled like lavender. It wasn't overpowering, but it was there, stronger by the air vents. This place spared no expense. I sipped my coffee and thought of Mary struggling to raise Keeper on her own, a special child she would forever be responsible for. The bartering and selling of her tonics and herbs to make a living. Would their life have been different if Katherine and Victor Dupree knew about their grandson?

"I thought we'd talk in one of the sitting rooms before I take you to Momma, if that's okay with you."

"That's fine." It was actually a good idea. I could gauge how willing the family would be to help by Belinda's responses.

Belinda pushed through French doors that opened into a solarium. Gas logs flickered with fake flames in a stone fireplace that occupied an entire wall. Love seats and wingback chairs in rich upholstery were strategically placed to encourage conservation, yet separated enough to ensure privacy. Belinda tucked herself into a corner of one of the love seats and waved her hand for me to join her.

She tucked her hair behind an ear, exposing thin streaks of gray mingled throughout the dark auburn waves. "What can I tell you about Kenny?"

I took my notebook from my bag. "Do you mind if I take notes?"

"Not at all. You might have to be selective with Momma's quotes, though. She's got a mouth on her worse than a sailor's."

My eyes flew wide with the sheer thought of the woman cursing up a blue streak. "Thanks for the warning," I said and smiled. On any given day, I could probably compete with her.

"Funny thing is it didn't start until a few years ago. It's embarrassing when the ladies from the church come to visit." Belinda laughed and I liked her. She seemed to have her act together.

I flipped to a blank page, pen poised. "So...about your brother. Let's start with a little history first. When did y'all leave Jackson Creek?"

"Right after Kenny graduated in 1967. Daddy had already moved and started his new job, but Momma didn't want to make Kenny start a new school halfway through his senior year."

Images of the class ring floated through my mind. *KJD and MAM*. Years of dirt and weathered earth clinging to the tiny etchings. "Did Kenny move to Knoxville with you?"

"Not really." She opened her hands like it would help her explain. "He joined the army right after graduation so, technically, he moved to Fort Bragg, North Carolina. When he came home on leave, he came to Knoxville."

That was why the newspaper articles listed him from Knoxville rather than Jackson Creek. Made sense. "When did he leave for Vietnam?"

Her mouth scrunched as she thought about it. "I'm not sure exactly. Momma can probably tell you. I know he was discharged in 1969, but he never came home. But you knew that already." She smiled warmly.

"Can you tell me what happened with that? What you remember about it?"

Belinda shifted on the small sofa, pulled one long leg up and tucked it underneath her bottom. Although in her late sixties, she moved with ease and grace. "I just remember Momma crying a lot. That's what I remember the most. I'll never forget the sound, especially when she thought me and my other brother, Russell, couldn't hear."

"Did your parents tell y'all anything, or did they try and keep it from you?"

"We didn't have family conversations about it if that's what you mean. It wasn't like they tried to hide anything, you know? They talked openly about it but never sat us down and said, 'look this is what's going on.' Daddy was really frustrated with the army and the State Department. I remember *that*."

I took a drink of coffee and collected my thoughts. Took a breath before proceeding. "Belinda, Kenny had a girlfriend in Jackson Creek—"

"Yeah, ah...I think her name was Mary."

My heart smiled in a teeny way for Mary. Maybe she mattered more than she thought she did. "Mary McCarter."

Belinda pointed a finger at me. "That's it. I knew it was something Scottish, Irish sounding. Whatever happened to her? Do you know?"

I held onto the truth. Somehow I didn't see Belinda Dupree, despite her friendliness, understanding the life of a granny witch. Maybe Aaron's documentary wasn't such a bad idea. Judging from Belinda's casualness about her brother's girlfriend, everything in me screamed the Duprees knew nothing about Keeper.

I moved on without acknowledging Belinda's question. I did acknowledge my dual purpose for being there. "Belinda—a few days ago, human remains were found in a field near the old mill. There's evidence that it might be your brother."

She blinked. Frowned. More from confusion than anger. At least I hoped. "I'm sorry—I don't think I understand what you just said."

I took the picture of the facial reconstruction from my bag, unfolded it, then handed it to her. "This is just a preliminary facial reconstruction of the skeleton. It's almost identical to his—"

"Yearbook picture." Her hand flew to her mouth as if to hold in a gasp. "It...can't be. He never came home."

She unfolded her legs and stood up, moving slowly away from the love seat. "He never came home. How is this possible?" She spun around to face me, jabbing a finger at the picture, emphasizing each word. "He (jab) did (jab) not (jab) come home."

"Belinda, there's only one way to know for sure. Your mother would be the closest DNA match possible. If it's a match, there's no doubt."

She shoved the picture at me. "No. I won't put her through that again."

My heart dropped like a weighted anchor. I wasn't expecting that response. Why would they not want to know?

"It would bring her closure. After all these years. She would finally know."

"She would know what? That her son came home and never told her?"

Mary shared the same sentiment. "So it would be better to let her keep thinking he's still alive living in the jungle on another continent? There's no closure in that, either."

She collapsed into one of the nearby chairs, looking more weary than put together like before. She fiddled with one of her earrings, unknowingly. Nervous habit. "There is no closure in any of it. Just more questions."

I scrambled for something to convince her. I sat on the edge of the love seat, like a cat ready to spring into action. "But these questions might finally lead to answers. *That* could bring your mother peace."

"She is at peace. She accepted Kenny wasn't coming home fifty years ago."

"But don't you think she deserves to know what happened?"

She leaned forward, burying her head in her hands. I thought she might be crying but when she looked up, there were no tears. Just a steel look of determination. "What if it turns out not to be my brother? Then what? She goes through the hurt all over again."

"But what if it is?"

Belinda stared at me then turned to the fire flickering in the fireplace. "How long have the remains been there?" Her voice was softer now, more reflective.

"We don't know for sure. We have reason to believe around forty-eight, forty-nine years."

She nodded slowly. "When he was supposedly discharged."

"Yes."

She closed her eyes, shrinking into her thoughts.

Although I wanted to leave here today with a swab from the inside of her mother's mouth, I was willing to come back if necessary. "Maybe this is something you want to talk over with your brother, Russell."

Belinda slowly shook her head. "He's not involved in anything to do with Momma. We don't speak."

"He doesn't visit?"

A laugh escaped and she apologized. "I'm sorry. It's really more sad than funny. But no, he doesn't visit. He's angry because this is where Momma chose to live." She gazed around the room, sweeping her hand at the finery. "It's not cheap and he sees it as his inheritance going down the drain."

"I'm sorry," I said truthfully.

"He wrote her off and she wrote him off. Both too stubborn for their own good."

Another family with severed ties, stained by the blood that bound them. "Maybe finally putting Kenny to rest could help them reconnect." I was reaching to keep the possibility alive. "She's lost both sons. Giving one a final resting place could bring her peace."

Belinda scrubbed her face with her hands, gazed at the fire. Her expression softened. I gave her time. My heartbeat matched each ticking second. When she finally spoke, she spoke in a slight voice. "How did he die?"

I matched my tone to hers. "There's evidence he was

murdered."

She jerked her head up, locking her eyes onto mine. "Murdered? Oh my God."

"I'm so sorry, Belinda. Unfortunately, that's what we've been able to gather so far."

Her brows knitted with questions. "What was he doing in Jackson Creek?"

My guess it had something to with Mary McCarter. I kept that feeling to myself. "We don't know yet. All we can do is speculate. Maybe visiting an old friend before coming back to Knoxville?"

Maybe he'd come back to surprise Mary? Meet his son? But Mary said he stopped returning her letters. She'd assumed he'd moved on, broken up with her in the most heartbreaking way. Why else would he return to Jackson Creek? The romantic in me saw a truly tragic love story. Two teenagers separated by a war, bound together forever through a child. The realistic side of me saw a seventeen-year-old in "trouble" with a jerk of a baby-daddy who cut her off to escape his responsibility.

Belinda reached for the picture again, studied it more thoughtfully this time. "Are the police investigating it as a murder?"

"Yes. It's being investigated by the Jackson County Sheriff's Department."

She slowly nodded then looked at the thin bangle watch circling her wrist. "It's almost noon. Momma should be finished with lunch and back in her room. I can introduce you if you'd like."

I finally relaxed enough to release a deep breath. "I'd like that very much."

CHAPTER 23

At ninety-two, Kathrine Dupree had a powerful presence. Above the maladies of old age, she still moved with grace, though maybe a little slower than she had in her youth. Her body had yet to give in to the usual signs of aging—stooped posture, lack of height. She carried her five-foot-eight-inch frame upright and tall. Her hair, still thick and wavy, was as white as freshly fallen snow.

I wondered why she was here. The woman arguing with Belinda yesterday about pears over peaches couldn't have been this woman.

Her room resembled a studio apartment without the kitchen. A sitting area sported a recliner and loveseat, end table with a lamp and vase of fresh flowers. A small coffee table with a stack of magazines sat in front of the loveseat. The bed, a standard queen, was tucked behind a ceiling-mounted sliding curtain along with a full-size dresser and mirror.

Dressed in a fashionable jogging suit, a hint of rose-colored lipstick brightening her smile, Katherine eyed me as Belinda made introductions. She claimed the recliner then motioned us to the loveseat. "Jackson Creek has a newspaper?"

"Yes, ma'am. Been in business fourteen years."

Katherine continued to watch me. "It's a nice little area. We probably wouldn't have left if my husband hadn't been transferred." She lifted a tea cup from the end table and took a sip. "Can I offer you some tea?"

"I'm fine, thank you." A gracious host, even in a nursing home. I liked this woman. I could also see how a pregnant teenager could have been terrified of her.

"So...Miss Logan...what can I do for you?"

Belinda and I looked at one another. I let her take the lead. Her mother never once lost her composure. Her expression never wavered as Belinda told her everything I had shared. When she was through, Katherine studied me until it became uncomfortable. I feigned interest in my nails so I could look away from the scrutiny.

"How was my son murdered?"

The suddenness of her question startled me, the intensity of her voice intimidating. I fought through the trepidation for Mary's sake. "He was shot in the head."

Belinda squeezed her hands together until her knuckles were white. Her diamond wedding band cutting into her skin. It was the first time she'd heard the cause of her brother's death.

Katherine never flinched. She did look away from me, turning her gaze to the colorful flowers on the end table. "Two tours in Vietnam and he's murdered in Jackson Creek, North Carolina."

I understood the irony of the final outcome that marred Kenny Dupree's life. By the grace of God surviving the hell of war only to be shot dead in your own backyard.

"Are you sure it's him?"

I started to speak but Belinda turned to me, cutting me off.

"Show her the picture."

Once again, I pulled the folded paper from my bag. Rather than opening it myself, I reached across Belinda and handed it to her mother. "It's a preliminary facial reconstruction," I explained.

Katherine opened the paper and for the first time since I'd been there, her expression changed. Her lips pulled into a tiny smile as she ran a finger over the face of her son. Her eyes glistened with tears.

"It looks just like his senior picture, doesn't it?" Belinda said.

Katherine nodded, still tracing her finger over the picture. "What made y'all think it was Kenny to begin with?"

"There was a class ring from 1967 found with the remains. It had initials engraved that matched his and...his girlfriend's."

"Mary McCarter," Katherine said, so matter of fact that it threw me.

"Yes, Mary."

"My husband didn't want him to have initials engraved in the ring. He said it was fine to have his own, but not a girl's."

Any girl's or just Mary's? "He didn't care for Mary?"

She smiled and wiped the back of her hand across her cheek, removing the single tear. "My husband could be an ass sometimes."

Belinda whipped her head around and stared at her mother.

Katherine waved her off. "Oh, relax. You know it's true. He was a good man, but he had his faults. He didn't accept a lot of things about that generation. He thought Mary was a hippie. The free love and drugs and music that wasn't Conway Twitty. He wanted no part of it."

I remembered Mary in her Rolling Stones t-shirt, barefoot, hair pulled into a braid. I wondered if Victor Dupree ever took the time to get to know her? If he ever knew of her kindness, her gentle nature?

Katherine placed the picture on the coffee table, face up, the hooded eyes gazing back at her. She took a sip of tea, collecting her thoughts. "We contacted Mary when Kenny never came home. She said she hadn't heard from him. Do you think she was involved with his death?"

Although when narrowing down a reason Kenny Dupree died from a bullet to the head, a jilted lover would be considered ample motive, I knew in my heart Mary McCarter wasn't involved. "No. Mary wasn't involved. She was devastated to learn he was in Jackson Creek and hadn't contacted her."

"I guess we have that in common."

She wanted to know details of the investigation, how the body was discovered, Dr. Scranton's involvement. And how we would move forward. "Are there any suspects?"

I withheld the information Calvin had revealed from them. It wasn't my place to give those details. "The sheriff has a few leads he's looking at." I left it at that.

"Why was he at that old mill? I don't think he knew anybody that worked there."

Belinda said, "Maybe one of his school buddies went to work there instead of going into the service?"

Katherine slowly shook her head. "We checked with everyone he knew—or at least that *we* knew he was friends with."

"Apparently they weren't very good friends if they killed him," Belinda said.

There was more truth in that than she knew. The man who

Calvin saw shoot Kenny was probably nothing more than an acquaintance. But how? A rival for Mary's affection? To my knowledge, Mary had never been involved with anyone. It added to the mystique that swirled around her. Keeper was obvious proof she'd had a relationship. But was there more than one?

"What do we do now?" Katherine said.

Belinda looked back and forth between me and her mother. "We let the sheriff's department do their investigation, I guess."

Katherine took the picture from the table and stared at it, her hand beginning to tremble. "Can I keep this?"

"Of course. And I'll make sure you're updated with any new developments."

Katherine nodded. "Please do. I wish there was something I could do to help."

I eyed the tea cup on the end table. The subtle rose-colored lipstick stain around the rim. "Actually, there is."

I handed the paper bag with the tea cup to Grayson then followed up with a kiss. "You can thank me later."

He was on the sofa in the sunroom reviewing Dr. Scranton's summary. It was after eight and I'd just gotten home. He'd picked Ivy up from Doretha's, helped Emma with her homework, fed the kids and himself—and even saved a plate for me. I couldn't remember why I'd been mad at him.

He peered into the bag. "You know it probably won't stand up in court."

I curled into him and rested my head on his shoulder. "Probably not but it will answer the question of his identity."

"True."

I told him everything about my visit to Knoxville, including the high-dollar nursing home. "When it comes time to put me away, please put me there."

He laughed and it made me smile. I loved his laugh. It was so sincere. "Only if we can get a double room," he said and that made me smile more.

A double room. A future. Not that I wanted to rush moving into a nursing home with him, but the thought of making the living arrangements official didn't bother me as much as it once did. He was great with the kids—and they adored him in return. He toted Ivy around like she was as much his as she was mine.

Our jobs were just a fact of our lives, of our relationship, we'd have to deal with. There would always be conflict over the public's right to know and their need to now. Conflict over information he couldn't reveal to me. The legal reasons we had to tread carefully.

Nothing that couldn't be conquered if we loved one another. And I did love him and he loved me. We'd make it work.

"Thanks for taking care of the kids," I whispered.

"No problem. Ivy's getting a little congestion in her nose."

Great. If it was coupled with another ear infection, her doctor would want me to consider ear tubes.

"And I had a talk with Cole."

I raised up and pulled away from him, staring into those baby blues as if I hadn't heard him right. "About the condom?"

"No, about football. Of course about the condom." He pulled me back to him and kissed my forehead. "I hope it was okay."

I didn't know what to say. Part of me was relieved he'd had a conversation I didn't want to have. The other part, the single mother in me, itched with control issues. Maybe if I'd known he was going to talk to him, I would have prepared myself better. Given up a little bit of the control I clung to.

I pushed aside the glitch and settled beside him again. "What did he say?" I quickly changed my mind and added, "No don't tell me. I'd rather not know. Maybe. Okay, what'd he say?"

Grayson laughed and I could feel the vibration in his chest.

"You can relax. Paisley told him no."

I turned and stared at him, relieved beyond measure. It wasn't that I thought ill of such a sweet girl, I just couldn't move past the teenagers in love scenario. "Seriously?"

He nodded, grinning. "She told him she wasn't ready. She didn't even know he was carrying around a condom. When he made his move and she shut him down, he didn't know what to do with it since he'd already opened it. He couldn't put it back in the nightstand, so he threw it in the burn pile."

Although a serious issue, I couldn't stop the giggle. "Can you imagine the panic he must have felt?"

"That probably wasn't all he was feeling."

I giggled even more. "She really is a special girl. I like her even more now."

I thought of Katherine Dupree's husband and how he had judged Mary and the only thing Mary was guilty of was loving Kenny. I didn't want to do that with Paisley. She was a nice girl, aside from that one little issue. I'd come to terms with it sooner or later.

Pushing the thoughts of teenage love to the back of my mind, I peered around Grayson's shoulder at Felicia's report. There was still a murder to contend with. "Anything new?"

"Looks like the bullet entered right above the left ear toward the back of the skull. Pretty consistent with what Calvin Lee said."

My heart stuttered in my chest. I didn't want to withhold anything from Grayson, but if I told him the truth about Calvin, he'd be legally bound to act on it. By telling him what I had already, I'd opened the doors to a very sticky situation.

"No exit wound," he continued. "All the damage was done on the inside of the skull."

"So he probably died instantly?"

"Probably."

There was always some comfort in knowing the victim didn't suffer. My Tommy had bled out. As blood drained from his shredded aorta, life drained from him. I always wondered what those last few minutes were like. Did he think of me and the kids? Did he know he was dying? Was he aware of the noises around him, of the smells?

I wondered, if in that split second between life and death, if Kenny Dupree thought of Mary.

CHAPTER 24

The next morning, after dropping Ivy off, I checked in at the office. Quinn was already there with the coffee on and a fire going in the old wood stove. I fixed us both a cup of coffee— Quinn's all trendy with caramel and sea salt creamer—and carried them into the work zone. He shoved another piece of wood into the stove, slammed the iron door closed, then accepted the mug.

Quinn blew into his coffee before taking a sip. "Lots of talk 'round town about the skeletal remains."

Although I was directly involved in the discovery and now the investigation—and knew the facts, the gossip of a small town fascinated me. "What are they saying?"

He lifted one shoulder in perfect harmony with the same corner of his mouth. "Nothing unusual but there was one theory I found interesting. You know that mill was ripe with accidents, right?"

I didn't know that but given the era, it wasn't surprising. The Occupational Safety and Heath Administration, or OSHA, wasn't founded until 1971 so worker safety wasn't the concern then that it is now. "A lot of mills had lax safety rules back then.

I don't think Jackson Creek Dye Mill was any different."

"Yeah, but think about this—OSHA was just being developed and the mill owners were feeling threatened. What if there'd been an accident, near life threatening but the person's still breathing. Rather than face all the scrutiny, and financial ruin, of a work-related death, the managers just take matters into their own hands."

I nearly choked on my coffee. "And what? Drug him out back and shot him like they were putting down a dog? Quinn...seriously?"

"You don't think it could have happened?"

"No. An industrial accident and cover up, yes. But the guy had a bullet in his head. And that's not necessarily public knowledge so keep that part quiet."

Quinn laughed, throwing his head back. "Oh, it's public knowledge. The fine folks of Jackson Creek just don't know the caliber."

The *Jackson Creek Chronicle* seldom broke the news, but we did confirm it. The life of a small-town newspaper.

Quinn carried his coffee to his desk. "So what is the latest?"

I wasn't ready to give up the warmth from the stove just yet. "We're fifty-fifty on the identity. We've narrowed it down to two possibilities. At least we think so."

"Are they using DNA?"

I nodded but before I could explain further, my cell phone buzzed from my pocket. It was Grayson calling from his office phone. I quickly answered. "Hey. What's up?"

"Got the results from Noreen Naylor's DNA sample."

I took a deep breath and steadied myself. "And?"

"Can you come to the office?"

"I'm on my way." I hurried back to the break room, dumped

the rest of my coffee, then rushed out.

Traffic moved in slow motion as I wasted no time getting to the sheriff's office. Even got honked at once for cutting in front of someone driving a tiny Smart car. I'd apologize later.

Again, I rushed by Annie without even as much as a slight wave. In Grayson's office, I wasn't terribly surprised to see Dr. Scranton standing behind his desk.

Fingers crossed, I hoped beyond measure the remains came back as Kelvin's. I'd hate it for Noreen, but could breathe so much easier knowing Mary's heart wouldn't have to be broken again.

Dr. Scranton smiled. "You're not going to believe this."

"It's a match?"

"Oh, it's a match alright." Grayson turned his monitor around again so I could see it.

An image of an older man stared back at me. An artist recreation rather than a photograph. I wasn't sure what I was looking at. "It looks like a courtroom sketch."

"Nope," Dr. Scraton said. "This—thanks to you—is my first hit on NameUs.gov."

I was happy for her, but I still wasn't sure what I was looking at. Or who. "Kelvin Dennis?"

Dr. Scranton was almost giddy. "Yes! Died in 2015 in a car accident in Wheeling."

I looked at Grayson, unsure how or what I felt. Numb only partially described it.

He read my confusion. "Noreen's DNA matched an unidentified accident victim in the NameUs database."

I sat down in the guest chair, trying to understand. NameUs was the government clearinghouse for missing and unidentified persons. I'd never had the opportunity, or reason, to use it but had heard about it through Grayson.

I'd told Noreen it could take months to get the results back. "How did you get a response so quickly?"

"Luck." Dr. Scranton handed me a folder with a couple pages of printouts. "I don't know how scientific you want to get in the newspaper but that's the test results. The bottom line is Mr. Dennis is not our victim. He died in Wheeling, West Virginia with no identification."

"But it was a car wreck, right? Wouldn't there be DMV records, VIN numbers, and a license plate registration?"

Grayson quickly shook his head. "He was hit by a car walking along the highway. No one in town or the surrounding area had ever seen him before."

"They classified him as a John Doe." Dr. Scranton added. "The same as our own John Doe."

I had a horrible, sinking feeling that we knew our John Doe's name. And Keeper was friendly with his killer.

Questioning Keeper on who he was with at the hardware store might scare him into thinking he'd done something wrong. That was the last thing I wanted to do. When Keeper thought he was in trouble he clammed up. Human nature. You either shut down or tell all. Rather than going to Keeper, I'd go around him.

Jimmy Pike had owned the hardware store for as long as I could remember. If I'd ever wished upon a star, or made a wish as I blew out birthday candles, I wished now that Jimmy would be able to name the mystery man.

Jackson Creek Hardware was about a mile outside of the town limits, still on the main road, but away from constraining zoning regulations. A sprawling two acres full of lumber, rolled fence, baled pine needles and corded firewood surrounded the cinder block building with windows so dusty you couldn't see through the glass. The store carried everything from nails to rat poison to toilet paper. The inside was just as cluttered as the outside. You'd often have to step over something or turn sideways to get through the aisles. The jangle of wind chimes was a sure sign someone had bumped into the metal tree display.

I wondered what the mystery man had bought when he came in, when he had Keeper with him? I hoped he was enough of a regular Jimmy would know his name.

If the number of cars in the gravel parking lot was any indication, even at this early hour, the store was hopping busy. Most weren't there to buy. They were there for the free coffee and gossip. The group of regulars, mostly retired old-timers, moved from the gas station up the road when the owner started charging for coffee. Now they met each morning at Jackson Creek Hardware to discuss the weather, world affairs, and sports scores. There were always a couple issues of the *Chronicle* in the vicinity to entice chatter.

I parked between two trucks and rushed inside to escape the cold. Christmas bells over the door, no matter the season, jingled with each new arrival. A group of men, including Pudge Collins, crowded around a stained coffee pot in the corner, away from the clutter of the rest of the store.

"There's my rabbit hunting buddy." Pudge lifted his disposable cup in my direction. "Great article in the paper about those bones."

The others agreed, nodding, and lifting their own cups. I was the toast of the hardware store.

"Know anything new?" Bartlett Joyce asked. His winter

beard touched his chest, full of gray wiry hair and God knows what else.

"Nothing new yet," though they knew I was lying.

Jimmy Pike topped off Pudge's coffee then carried the empty carafe behind a door with a lopsided "Employees Only" sign. He came back with fresh water to make another pot. "Hey Ava," he said and smiled, exposing the black hole where a tooth used to be. "What can I help you with today?"

"I was wondering if I could talk to you a minute, Jimmy."

He dried his hands on his heavy, thermal-lined jeans. "Reckon so."

I purposely moved toward the sales counter, away from the coffee club, hoping Jimmy would follow my lead. He glanced back at the crowd then moved behind the counter. "Everything okay?" he said tentatively.

"Oh, sure. I just wanted to ask you a couple questions about someone who shops with you."

He glanced again at his buddies then nodded nervously. I understood now why Jimmy Pike had earned the nickname Nervous Nelly.

"I'm looking for the name of a man who's been here in the past with Keeper McCarter. The man may be in his sixties now, maybe even seventy."

"Know what he looks like?"

"Not really. Just an average looking guy." It sounded lame. So hopeless. I came close to apologizing to him for asking something so silly, something so un-answerable.

He called over to his buddies, "Any of you know a guy that hangs around with Keeper?"

"Keeper McCarter?" Bartlett Joyce said, like there was really more than one Keeper in Jackson Creek.

"Yes. That Keeper." I smiled. So much for speaking with Jimmy confidentially.

"He comes in sometimes with the guys from the fire department," Jimmy said. "I think the fire chief lets him work there some."

I knew everyone at the fire department and there wasn't anyone in the same age range as the suspect. Not even remotely close.

"I've seen him tool 'round town some with Roy," Pudge said.

Jimmy bobbed his head up and down in a nervous nod. "Yeah—he's been in here a couple times with Roy, come to think of it."

If Roy McCarter wasn't Keeper's uncle, I'd raise an eyebrow. As it were, after Mary's father died, Roy filled those shoes. It was natural for Keeper to tag along with him.

Bartlett Joyce tossed his cup in the trash. Adjusted his wool cap. "Thanks for the coffee, Jimmy. I guess I need to get on to work. You boys hold down the fort."

"Get to work?" Pudge said, letting lose with a belly-jarring guffaw. "Ain't worked a day in your life."

The men all shared a hearty laugh, including Bartlett Joyce. Two of the other men tossed their cups, too, and also headed out.

I hesitated a moment, not wanting to leave yet. The only name I'd managed to get out of anyone was Roy McCarter. There had to be another name, someone Mary was comfortable enough with to trust with her son.

With just Pudge, me and Jimmy left, Pudge refilled his cup and offered to fix one for me. I waved him off and asked about Tucker, the wayward beagle. The one who began all this.

"With a little more training, he might be all right." Pudge laughed. If anyone would know, it would be Pudge. I owed the man an article.

Jimmy stopped tidying up the coffee area long enough to join the conversation. "Might make a good cadaver dog."

"I hadn't thought of that," Pudge said.

I added, "I know the DEA is using beagles and bloodhounds for drug work, too. So is the ATF for explosives."

Pudge sipped his tar-black coffee. "Only problem with that is I'd have to give up the little guy and I've grown kinda fond of the little shit."

We laughed and I remembered how Pudge picked Tucker's bark out of the pack. Knew the little "shit's" howl from a distance.

I listened to them chat back and forth, arguing about different dog breeds and their specialties, while Jimmy straightened one spot in the mess of the whole store. With inventory spilling from every corner, except the coffee corner, maybe it was the only area he felt he had control over.

Glancing around the store, familiarity brushed over my heart. Dust an inch thick clung to a red plastic hummingbird feeder. The wind chimes had hung on that metal tree so long the chimes had tarnished. Knowing a killer had walked in here with Keeper, probably stood where I stood now, made me angry.

Jimmy made no effort to straighten anything else. "Hear tale ol' man Briscoe has a new litter of border collies he's selling for dang near a thousand bucks a piece."

Pudge nearly choked on his coffee. If I'd been drinking, I would have. "A thousand dollars? For a border collie?" Pudge gasped.

"Oh, he'll field train 'em before he let's 'em go. Good

working dog—a good herding dog, worth every penny."

As a proud owner of a border collie, I had to agree with Jimmy. Although Finn was more couch potato than working dog, she had taken to herding Boone the cat. Or trying to.

Pudge and Jimmy had gone from dogs to trucks and had circled back to the old mill. While I moved carefully around the store, watching my step, taking it all in and wondering if Aaron could accurately grasp the sentiment within these walls, I caught snippets of conversation.

"How long you reckon that old mill's been closed?" Jimmy said.

"July 3rd, 1988." I remembered the date Grayson quoted from earlier, the date apparently etched into his memory. Now mine as well.

I thought of Grayson's father digging coal to support his family. Grayson watching him die, no longer able to breathe. It wasn't that unusual around here. Especially the deeper you went into Appalachia. Still a tragedy, no matter how commonplace it had become.

Jimmy and Pudge stared at me, probably wondering how I knew the exact date.

I offered a tiny smile. "Research."

Pudge nodded, understanding "research."

Jimmy said, "Sure did put a lot of people out of work. I don't know if we ever did recover from it."

"We recovered," I said, quick to defend the area. I winked at Jimmy. "We created our own jobs like newspapers and hardware stores."

Jimmy wiped the same spot again on the glass counter top with a dirt-covered rag. "That's true, I guess. Sure don't pay like mill work, though."

We all laughed at the truth. Back in the day, if you were lucky enough to get on at a mill, you were set for life.

Jimmy stopped his cleaning and stared at Pudge. "Hey, Pudge—didn't Roy McCarter used to work at the mill?"

CHAPTER 25

I left the hardware store with my heart pounding, my thoughts a jumbled mess. *Clarity.* I needed to get my thoughts together and talk to Mary with a clear head. I fought the temptation of rushing straight over there and confronting her with the information. This would be life-changing for Mary on so many levels, and I needed to act rationally, not with my usual impulsiveness. I headed home, grabbed my winter hiking gear and Finn then traipsed down to the river. I needed the soul-searching clarity only the river could provide.

Ice crystals glistened on the rocks poking above the rushing water. I walked along the bank with purpose. With temperatures in the upper twenties, I didn't have time to sit and ponder. Each step pushed a little bit of clutter from my thoughts. Finn walked ahead of me, venturing off the trail in spots. I watched her stick a paw in the water, testing. She quickly stepped back and high-tailed it up the bank to join me.

Was Roy McCarter the man Calvin saw kill Kenneth Dupree? Calvin had no reason to point a finger at Roy unless it was true. He didn't even know Roy's name, just that he'd seen him with *that simple-minded fella.*

But if it was true, why? Why would Roy resort to killing Mary's boyfriend? And how did he know when Kenny would be there? Unless Mary was involved?

No—absolutely not. I couldn't even fathom that to be true. A winter wind rustled through the bare trees, stinging my raw cheeks. I pulled the wool scarf tighter around my neck and tucked it deeper into my coat. My eyes watered from the cold. Crazy, I knew, being out in weather like this but the river was my think tank. Some people did their best thinking in the shower. I did mine on the banks of Jackson Creek.

Was it a family honor thing? Had Roy killed Kenny because Mary was pregnant? How silly and archaic. Jackson Creek might be deep in the Appalachia Mountains, but it wasn't in the stone age. Even if he had—again, how did he know Kenny would be there? *That* was the key. If Mary wasn't involved, was her father? And again, how did *he* know? The line circled right back to Mary.

I caught myself on the verge of tears and it had nothing to do with the freezing temperature. What if Mary was involved? What would happen to Keeper? What would happen to Calvin when his truth was exposed? There was so many people this could affect and there were no happy endings for anyone.

The only thing I was a hundred percent sure of was I needed to talk to Mary.

I took my phone out and checked the signal. Two bars. I stared at the phone, punched in Grayson's number but didn't hit "Call." After a long hesitation, I typed out a text: *New development. Going to Mary's.*

The phone dinged an acknowledgement when I hit "Send."

"Come on Finn." I called her to me then headed back to the house, anxious to discover the truth.

Shortly after, the Tahoe dipped down into the holler where Mary and Keeper lived. On days like today, the sun struggled to crest the surrounding peaks, casting an even deeper chill on the valley than a thermometer could reflect. White smoke rose from the chimney, thick as the clouds. Wind blew the remaining dead and crinkled leaves into spinning clusters.

Keeper didn't rush out to greet me this time. It was silly, I knew, but I wanted to believe he'd be happy to see me even after today. It was the wind chill and the freezing temperatures keeping him inside, I told myself.

I doubled-up on the lip balm then climbed out of the Tahoe. I carefully navigated the front steps. Black ice not yet touched by the warmth of the sun spotted the wooden steps, keeping them slick in spots. As soon as I lifted my hand to knock, the door opened and Keeper met me with a tight embrace.

"Momma—Ava's here." He all but lifted me and carried me inside like a doll he was afraid to let go of. "Momma, look, it's Ava."

"I see that son. Let her get in and close the door." She smiled apologetically. There was no need. I accepted her son for what he was. A kind and sweet man.

With the wood-burning stove pumping out the heat, the house was toasty warm. A cluster of cinnamon sticks stood at attention in a mug of water on the cast-iron stove. I stripped out of my heavy coat, scarf and gloves and dropped them across an empty quilt rack Mary used for that purpose. In the spring and summer, it held the quilts she'd made. In the fall and winter, the quilts went on the beds and the winter gear hung across the spindles instead. There was so much comfort inside the walls of the old house, I hated myself for bringing pain into it.

"Is this a social visit?" Mary said, probably already knowing the answer. The concern showed in her face.

I glanced at Keeper who had retreated to *his* chair with an Early Reader book. *Biscuit Takes a Bath.* I'd read the same book to Ivy night after night. Keeper moved his finger along the words as he silently recited each one.

"He's learning," Mary whispered. "Come on in the kitchen. We can talk in there."

"How long has he been learning?"

"For a while now I guess. He has picture books, but he said he wanted to read the letters. I bought a stack of those little "Biscuit" books at the flea market for him last Labor Day."

I sat down at the table while Mary put a kettle of water on the stove. A pot of pintos simmered on the back burner. She took two mugs from the cupboard slick with sweat. The heat from the wood stove combined with the cook stove nearly crossed the line from comfortable to suffocating.

Mary dropped two tea bags in the mugs then leaned against the counter, facing me, feet crossed at the ankles. Barefoot. "I noticed there wasn't a recipe in the paper this week."

Damn. Called out on that recipe again. "It'll be in the next one. I promise."

"I'll be glad to send you some if you'd like. I have all of Momma's cookbooks, plus all the homemade ones she jotted down on paper. A napkin, notebook paper, a get-well card. I keep saying one day I'm gonna organize them all." She smiled, tended to the tea when the kettle shrilled.

"Mary—"

"It was him, wasn't it?"

God—I didn't know how to have this conversation. My mind stumbled over what to say. There were still so many variables to the story, so many unanswered questions. The only thing I knew with any certainty, despite everything saying differently, was Mary was not involved in Kenny Dupree's death.

"We're waiting on confirmation to be a hundred percent positive."

She brought the two mugs to the table and sat across from me. "I guess I knew it when you showed me the picture. I just didn't want to accept it."

"You had no idea he was back in Jackson Creek?"

She shook head, so much more in control than she had been the other day. I imagined when she replaced the denial with reality, the calm set in.

"I went to Knoxville and met his mother and sister. They had no idea he was home, either."

"Belinda. She was nice. I only met her once, but I remember she was kind. I don't remember his mother's name." She took a sip of tea, eyes narrowed with memories.

"Katherine." I didn't tell her how Katherine described what her husband had said about Mary. I'm sure it wasn't news to her. Intuition, a sixth sense, whatever you wanted to call it, Mary didn't just know. She felt it.

She'd always told me the closer she was to a person, the less she could see, and this time it was clouded with closeness. Kenny...her brother...her son. "Do you know how he died?"

I wanted to tell her but stopped short. An inkling of suspicion? I brushed that thought away, knowing it just wasn't possible. I held back the truth for her own protection. "All we really know is he was killed."

She nodded, accepting it as the truth, but knowing I knew more. My mouth opened with "Roy" firmly on my tongue when Keeper bounded into the kitchen. "Look Momma, I can read this whole page."

He sat down beside her, his finger still tracing the words, and read aloud. Mary and I glanced at one another and smiled. The conversation could wait. Her eyes were wet, but she held the tears at bay as she watched Keeper's finger move along the letters.

"Now I can read the letters, can't I, Momma?"

"Yes, you can read the letters."

Keeper sprang up from the chair, almost knocking it backwards, and grabbed his jacket from the coat peg at the back door.

"Keeper, what are you doing?" Mary said, her face full of confusion.

"Getting the letters." He was out the back door before we could react. The screen door banged against the frame as it closed, offering little protection from the winter. Cold air rushed inside, overtaking the warmth.

"Keeper!" Mary leapt up and started after him but stopped at the screen door. "What is he doing?"

I rushed to join her. "Where'd he go?"

"He went in the barn. Crazy boy's gonna freeze to death."

I ran into the living room and grabbed my coat, pulled it on on my way out the back door. The wind bit at my cheeks and blew my hair into my eyes. I struggled against the cold, my lungs unable to take in the frigid air. I reached the barn and tugged the heavy door open. I yelled for him but it came out like a bark. "Keeper!" The piercing cold ripped at my throat.

"Up here."

There was movement in the upper loft.

"Keeper—come down. Come back inside. It's too cold to be out here." My teeth chattered noisily. I crammed my hands under my arms to protect my aching fingers. "Keeper, come on."

"I'm coming. I'm getting the letters."

"The what?" Wind howled outside and pushed its way through the cracks and crevices of the wood structure.

"The box of letters. I can read them now." He popped up in the loft, a green metal lockbox in his hands.

Chapter 26

The small key lock hung open, dangling from the metal box. I had a box just like it. Fireproof. Waterproof. It was my grab-and-go box of important documents. The kids' birth certificates and their immunization records, Tommy's death certificate. The deed to the house. The past.

Mary stared at the box now sitting on her table. "Keeper, where did you get this?"

"I found it up in the barn. I can read them now."

Read them? The letters—it wasn't the letters of the alphabet he wanted to read. It was actual letters.

"When did you find it?" Mary said.

Keeper shrugged. No big deal to him. The important part was whatever letters were in that box, he could read now. He removed the lock like a kid opening a treasure box. "A bunch of years ago. Uncle Roy told me not to tell anyone. He said it was a secret."

My chest tightened as thoughts slammed into my brain. I knew of one secret Roy McCarter had. Were there more?

Keeper flipped the box open excitedly and Mary gasped, pushing his hand away. A handgun lay on top of an array of envelopes. Keeper reached for the gun and casually lifted it out, giving no more thought to it than if he'd picked up a piece of discarded trash.

"Keeper—" Mary's voice hitched. "You have to be careful."

"It's okay, Momma. Uncle Roy let me hold it before he locked it up."

Heart pounding, a cold sweat trickled down my back. Keeper was holding the gun that killed his father. He set it down, more interested in the letters he wanted so badly to read. "Look, Momma. Look at all the letters."

Mary rifled through them, her eyes wide with shock. The envelopes were addressed to her. Return address *PFC Kenneth J Dupree*. Tears rushed from her eyes, spilling with confusion. "I don't...understand."

I grabbed an envelope, tore it open. Dated March 5, 1969. I read aloud:

Dear Mary,

I don't know what's happened and why you're not writing back anymore, but I do hope you're well. I understand if you've moved on. I can't say that I blame you. I still want to marry you and raise our little boy on a farm if you'll have me. I'm a changed man, Mary. The things I've seen over here are worse than any nightmare you can imagine. Maybe one day I'll tell you about it. Until then, I love you and Kenny Jr. Give him a kiss for me.

Kenny

I scrambled to open the next one. Hands shaking, I read it, too, aloud. My voice quivered with emotion.

Dear Mary,

I watched a buddy die today. It reminded me of that car wreck that boy from school was killed in. Remember that? I can't remember his name. Anyway, this isn't something I want to remember so it might be a good thing I can't remember it that well. Momma said Daddy's settled into his job now and working all the time, so she took up some kind of dance class at the community center. Imagine that! Is our little boy growing? I still haven't told Momma about him. I'm not trying to hide it, I just haven't found the right time to tell her she's a grandma. She may not take kindly to that! I love you, Mary. Give Kenny Jr. a big hug and a kiss.

Kenny

There were so many more. Stacks of emotion and love. Mary wept as I read each one, in order according to the dates. There were letters from Mary to him, too. No wonder he felt she'd moved on. The correspondence suddenly stopped. For both of them.

Either Roy or her father had intercepted the letters and stashed them away. I couldn't begin to understand the betrayal Mary felt at that moment. "Keeper, are these your Uncle Roy's or your grandpa's?"

"Uncle Roy said they was grandpa's but he was keeping 'em for him. Why are you crying, Momma?" He looked at her, those dark eyes full of concern. He then bounced up, disappeared into another room and returned with a handful of crumpled tissue. "This will make you feel better."

Mary accepted the offer and wiped her eyes as a tearful smile tried to make its way to the surface. "Thank you, boy." She sniffled then turned her red-streaked eyes to me. There was no smile or gratitude. Just a demand. "How did he die?"

"Mary—"

She slammed both hands on the table and shot up. Demanding and angry. "How'd he die, Ava? I know you know!"

Years, *decades*, of information had been withheld from her. I didn't want to withhold more. "He was shot in the head."

She collapsed in the chair, the sorrow so deep, so paralyzing to witness. Helpless, Keeper grabbed his mother and wrapped his arms around her. "It's okay, Momma."

He had no idea the scope of her pain, yet he wanted to offer comfort. He looked to me for guidance and all I could do was watch, shattered for the both of them. For Kenny Dupree.

When the sobs settled into acceptance, Mary wiped her face with her hands. She eyed the gun with a burning hatred. She knew. There was no need to match the bullet to the gun. "It was Daddy's gun."

"Mary, it wasn't your father who killed him."

"Roy?"

I nodded, accepting what Calvin had said as truth. Mary had yet to look away from the gun. "There's a witness who saw it happen."

Keeper looked at Mary, his brows knitted. "Who died, Momma? Saw what happen?"

Mary squeezed his hand. "Don't worry about it, son."

The tone of her voice didn't offer the usual comfort she was known for. It was alarming, setting off bells and whistles in my mind. My heart picked up speed. *Grab the gun. Grab it before she does.*

Just as I reached for it, Mary picked it up, checked the chamber. "Ava, will you stay with Keeper a few minutes?"

"Absolutely not. Mary, give me the gun." I reached for it but she pulled away.

"Where you going, Momma? Why can't I go?"

"I'll be back. You stay here with Ava." She jerked the truck keys from a catch-all bowl on the table and was out the door before I could stop her.

"Mary—don't!" I screamed, grabbing my phone, praying for a signal. One bar. Dammit!

I rushed outside with Keeper on my heels and dove into the Tahoe. Screaming at my phone. "Come on. I need a signal."

"Where'd my momma go, Ava?" Keeper fastened the passenger seatbelt.

I looked over the acreage. The rolling hills and valleys—suddenly aware I had no idea which way to Roy's. With all the cut-throughs and switchbacks, tractor roads and dirt trails, any one of them could lead to his place. "Do you know how to get your uncle's house?"

Keeper stared at me. Blank.

Dammit! I checked my phone again. Two bars. I typed out a text to Grayson and watched the little blue circle spin until I wanted to slam it against the steering wheel. The phone finally dinged, indicating the text was delivered. I scanned the area, looking for tire tracks, looking for exhaust, anything. She couldn't have gotten that much of a head start. We were right behind her.

I looked behind the Tahoe and there, right behind a cluster of pines, a road disappeared. I jammed the truck in reverse and backed up, then slammed it in drive and spun tires in the leftover snow.

Keeper grabbed the overhead handle, eyes wide with fear. "Momma don't like me going this fast, Ava."

The Tahoe bounced over gullies and rivets in the dirt road

and I never once hit the brakes. The suspension would need work when this was over. At the moment, it was the least of my concerns. I caught sight of the truck stopped in front of an old single-wide trailer. Like Mary, I didn't bother to park, just skidded to a stop and jumped out.

Please God, don't let me be too late.

I ran up on the porch and pushed the door open, praying like I'd heard Doretha pray. God, Grayson—anyone to stop this from happening.

My heart was beating so hard and loud, I could feel it in my ears. Mary stood in the living room, gun pointed center mass right at her brother. He was a sniffling little man and I was tempted to pull the trigger myself.

But I knew better. "Mary, don't do this. Give me the gun."

She didn't flinch. Never took her eyes off her brother. "I asked you to stay at the house with Keeper."

Keeper started around me, heading toward his mother, but I blocked him with my arm. He didn't object but was clearly confused. "Momma?"

"Ava, please take him home," Mary pleaded.

Roy had his trembling hands in the air, chest high. His mouth quaked with fear. Good. The only reason I didn't want Mary to shoot was because it would destroy her life and Keeper's.

"I trusted you with my son. And you took his father from him." Teeth clenched, Mary spit at her brother. So much hatred, so much venom.

"It was all Daddy's doing," Roy pleaded. "He was scared you'd leave him. He couldn't take care of Momma by hisself."

Mary flinched and tears flooded her eyes.

"But you did it, Roy. You pulled the trigger. Not Daddy."

"Don't you see Mary? He made me do it. He kept all those letters, never mailed the ones you wrote. He even made me write a letter—that last one—pretending I was you. Told Kenny to meet you at the mill. What day, what time. He made me make it sound like you was working at the mill and wanted to see him on break."

Mary's hands trembled, the rock steady facade beginning to crumble. "I loved him, Roy, and you took him from me. You took him from Keeper."

"You was seventeen years old. You got yourself knocked up with a half-wit child—"

The blast exploded, tearing through the wall and my eardrums. I jerked my hands over my ears, hoping to stop the ringing. It took me a second to realize what had happened and then I grabbed for Mary. "No!"

I slammed into her, knocking her off balance, the gun waving in the air. I wrestled it away from her while Roy cowered in the corner. "She tried to kill me! You saw it!"

I wrapped Mary in a tight hug, allowing her to fall into me. I'd be her support system as long as she needed. I glared at the sniffling, pathetic man squatting in the corner. "You're lucky I didn't have the gun. I wouldn't have missed."

CHAPTER 27

Roy was still shouting at Mary from the back of a squad car. Handcuffed and screaming that his sister should be the one arrested, not him. Still standing in the living room, I pulled a blanket from the creep's tattered sofa and wrapped it around Mary's shoulders. Her feet were still bare. Her teeth chattered.

Grayson studied the bullet hole in the wall. Only inches from the ceiling, it was evident Mary had aimed above Roy's head. At least that's how I hoped he saw it, too.

Keeper followed every step Grayson took, talking a mile a minute, explaining what happened. Grayson let him talk, with occasional glances to me for clarification.

"Can I take them back home?" I worried about Mary, barefooted, no coat.

Grayson had a deputy follow us in Mary's truck back to the house. With instructions to stay there until he finished at Roy's. There were questions to answer.

I got Mary settled on the sofa near the wood stove and wrapped her feet in hot towels. She still hadn't spoken. Keeper stayed beside her while I heated water for tea. I stirred the pintos, carrying on like it was any other cold winter day. As the tea kettle rumbled, I finally cried. My brain couldn't comprehend the pain and longing she'd lived with all these years. Thinking she was nothing more than a "teenage thing."

Things were different now than they were back then. Still, I was so thankful Paisley had told Cole she wasn't ready to take their relationship to the next level. Truth was, Cole wasn't as ready as his body thought he was, either. When the heart and body tag team against the brain, someone ends up hurt.

After wiping my eyes, I carried a steaming cup of tea into the living room and handed it to Mary. Keeper was still beside his mother on the sofa, so I sat in his chair. A stack of the little books lay on the floor beside the chair.

"Thank you." Mary's voice was tired, but the color was slowly returning to her cheeks.

"You're welcome, Momma." Keeper said it so proudly that Mary and I looked at one another and smiled just a little.

"Keeper, how did you know the box was there?" Mary said.

"Remember Blue, the chicken? She liked to roost up there." He told us about collecting four eggs from her in one day and how he busted one coming down the ladder. "I'm sorry, Momma. I tried to hang on to it. I shoulda put it in my pocket."

Then he told us about the snake that got Blue's other eggs and how the chicken squawked and carried on like he'd never seen. After another story about the chicken and with some gentle prodding from Mary, he circled back to the box.

"Uncle Roy was workin' on the tractor one day and I tolt him I'd seen that box and he tolt me to leave it be. He showed me the gun and said he had to hide it there so the bad guys won't never find it. Tolt me to help him keep it a secret."

Why would the SOB even show him the gun? I accepted that was one of those questions that may never be answered and

pushed it out of mind. Still, my disgust with Roy McCarter grew
with every passing minute.

"Secrets ain't good, are they Momma?"

Mary gently ran her hand over Keeper's hair. I imagined
her holding him as a baby, barely more than a baby herself,
twirling the curls around her finger. "No, Baby. Secrets ain't
good."

Keeper leaned into his mother, smiling broadly at me. He
giggled like a little school kid. "But I snuck some peeks at the
box when Uncle Roy weren't here. That's when I seen all the
letters."

Mary furrowed her brows, her lips puckered with questions.
"Keeper, how did you know what they were?"

He smiled, looking at Mary like he didn't understand what
she meant. "I watched *Blue's Clues*. They got a new letter every
day on the show."

My heart nearly burst and I wanted to wrap him in my
arms, cradle him like a child. But he wasn't a child, he was a
grown man with no idea how much he was loved.

Mary dabbed at her eyes. She shook her head and
mumbled, "A kid's television show."

Grayson knocked once on the front door then let himself in.

Keeper leapt up and rushed toward him. "Sheriff Ridge,
weren't my momma's fault. Weren't her fault 'tall."

Grayson clapped Keeper on the shoulder reassuringly.
"There's nothing to worry about, Keeper. We'll take care of it."

He went back to the sofa and sat beside Mary. "Did you
hear that, Momma? Sheriff Ridge is gonna take care it."

Keeper nodded like he was totally confident there was
nothing else to be concerned about. I looked at Grayson for my
own confirmation.

He knelt in front of Mary. "Feel up to telling me what happened?"

She turned her eyes downward like an embarrassed child. Like a seventeen-year-old with a baby on the way. It took her a moment to gather her thoughts. To tell her and Kenny's story. And their son's story.

A week had passed since Roy's arrest. Grayson gave Mary a lecture on firearm safety along with a date for target practice. I didn't think she needed it. She hit exactly where she'd aimed.

Roy, like the sniveling little pathetic man he was, confessed to Kenny's murder so there was no need for a trial, only a sentencing. Calvin's secret was safe with me. I honestly didn't know what I would have done if there had been a trial. Best not to think about it.

With Roy in jail, Grayson called us to his office. I met Mary and Keeper there and held Mary's hand as we walked down the hall. Keeper followed, asking if he could see the jail when we were through. Roy was still there, safely tucked away out of sight, out of mind, so I wasn't sure if giving Keeper the grand tour was smart.

"We'll see, Keeper." I offered the standard mother response when you need more time to come up with an excuse.

Mary glanced at me and smiled. She wore a heavy wool sweater over her Rolling Stones t-shirt, faded jeans with frayed hems, and clunky, surplus army boots. Her hair was gathered into a loose ponytail midway down her back. No makeup. No pretense. If she was a hippie, I wanted to be one when I grew up.

Grayson's door was open, so we went in. Dr. Scranton was in her familiar place, behind his desk looking at the computer.

Grayson didn't tell me the spunky doctor was going to join us. My eye twitched and I reminded myself this wasn't about me. Whatever irritation the doctor may have caused was childish. Let it go.

"Ava, hi," she said, smiling. "I didn't know you were coming. Did you get your little paper out?"

From behind his desk, Grayson shot up and motioned toward the guest chairs. "Thanks for coming down. I didn't want to tell you over the phone."

Tell us what? My stomach jumped with dread. A summons like that was never good. I reached over between the chairs and squeezed Mary's hand, steeling myself for the worst.

Forget Felicia Scranton.

Grayson came around to the front of his desk and leaned against it. I could usually read his expression, but not this time. "We got the results back from the DNA test. It was a match to Katherine Dupree's."

Although the news wasn't a surprise, Mary sucked in a sharp breath. The finality was both welcome and heartbreaking.

Keeper bent down between his mother and me. "What's that mean, Momma? What kind of test? I can take it if you want me to 'cause I can read now."

Mary smiled at him, ruffled his hair. "It's okay, son. It's not that kind of test. Thank you, Sheriff Ridge for letting me know."

"Sure. No problem." He dug the toe of his boot into the carpet, watching the rivet widen then narrow depending on how he moved his foot. "There is something else, Mary. Katherine Dupree is coming in to claim the remains. She wants to meet with you...and Keeper."

"That's me, Momma. Am I gonna get to meet someone new?"

Mary got up and moved around the room. Her face so full of confusion, it made my heart hurt. "You told her about Keeper?"

He cleared his throat. "I had to. She's not the only living relative."

"What about me?" Despite his childlike qualities, Keeper was growing irritated with all the talk going on about him.

"Honey, it's okay," Mary said. Her face wasn't as reassuring but luckily, Keeper was oblivious to such subtle signs.

"When are they coming?" I asked.

"Tomorrow. They've scheduled a private room at the funeral home. They want y'all to be there."

"A funeral?" Keeper scrunched his nose. "Who died? Who died, Momma?"

Mary sighed heavily, her shoulders seeming to drop to her knees. "Just a friend."

CHAPTER 28

The next day, I headed back to West Jefferson early enough to make the afternoon appointment with the Duprees. I'd promised Noreen Naylor closure and I was going to deliver. I'm sure the news about her brother wasn't what she'd want to hear, but it was probably what she suspected all along.

I had the artist sketch of John Doe tucked into my bag and walked tentatively to the deli section. Noreen was loading fresh-baked pastries from baking sheets into the display cabinet. The chocolate-glazed donuts and streusel-topped muffins looked and smelled delicious. Comforting.

Noreen glanced up at me and smiled. The smile quickly faded as she probably knew why I was back.

"Can you take a break?" My voice was soft, caring. Despite all that was wrong with Kelvin, he was her big brother.

She nodded then pushed open the swinging doors and told a co-worker she'd be right back. She took off her disposable gloves, finger-by-finger, then came around the counter and motioned to the tiny café.

We sat at the same small table as we had before. We didn't order coffee. We just sat there for a moment, silent. Me, not knowing exactly what to say, and Noreen not wanting to hear it.

She swallowed hard then straightened, shifting her weight. "Were those bones his?"

I shook my head. "Those weren't. But we did have a match."

Surprised, her eyes widened. "The DNA?"

"Yes. The sample they were able to extract from your cup matched an unidentified body found in Wheeling."

I took out the picture and handed it to her. Tears flooded her eyes as she ran a finger lightly over Kelvin's face. "What happened to him?"

"He was hit by car. It was late at night and he was walking on the highway. The driver did stop. They did try to help him."

She nodded, smiled slightly. "Weird, but that makes me feel a little better."

I reached out and took her hand. "It is comforting to know someone was there, trying to help him."

"Are you going to tell Shelly?"

Truthfully, I hadn't given it much thought. His sister, the one who loved him, was the one that came to my mind. Shelly, though, did deserve to know the man who'd sliced her throat open would never again be a threat. "She'll be notified."

Noreen refolded the picture. "Can I keep this?"

"Certainly. There's contact information on the back for the organization you need to contact to claim the remains."

She tucked the paper into the pocket of her blue smock and stood. A little wobblier than before, maybe a little older. "Thank you. At least now we know, right?"

Noreen headed back to the deli. Another long day ahead. But at least now she knew. Then why'd I feel so horrible?

* * *

In one of the parlor rooms of Creekside Funeral Home, Keeper frowned and tugged at the collar of his shirt. Top button closed, he fussed with it until Mary told him to stop.

"You look handsome, Keeper." He did and I wanted to let him know. I smiled at the unruly hair as Mary tried smoothing it. The more she brushed, the more waves were created.

"Who did we come to see, Momma?"

Mary chewed the inside of her gum, putting some thought into how she was going to answer. "Just someone who wants to meet you, that's all."

"Do I know 'em?"

Mary popped him lightly on the arm with the brush. "Silly. I said it was someone who wants to meet you so do you think you know them?"

He shook his head. "Guess not."

Mary gave up on his hair and tucked the brush into her bag. Her own hair hung loose today. A soft peasant blouse paired with a flowing maxi skirt gave her the look of a gypsy. Beautiful inside and out. I hoped Katherine Dupree would see that.

My own palms were moist with anticipation.

We'd waited about twenty minutes when finally, Grayson opened the door and escorted Katherine and Belinda into the parlor. Katherine leaned into a cane but still commanded attention. Dressed in a pant suit and pearls, she strode straight to Mary. Belinda walked over to me, arms outstretched for an embrace.

"So you're Mary McCarter," Katherine said. She shifted her cane from her right hand to her left, then offered the free one to Mary. "It's a pleasure to see you again. When was it last?

Graduation?"

The breath Mary had held for fifty years seeped out and brought with it a tiny smile. "Yes, it was graduation."

"I told Kenny that day to put a ring on it. I told him you were a keeper."

"No—I'm Keeper." Like a fine, well-bred gentleman, he offered his hand.

Katherine shook his hand then stepped back to get a better look at him. "My, my, my. A spitting image. And I agree. You are a keeper."

Keeper turned to Mary. "What does that mean, Momma?"

"It means I wouldn't give you up for the world."

Everyone laughed, even Keeper, although I suspected he had no idea why.

Katherine waved her cane toward one of the velvet upholstered couches. "Let's sit. My knees are wobbly." Belinda offered a supportive arm but Katherine shooed her away. After she settled into the soft cushion, she pointed at Grayson. "You, the handsome one, why don't you take the boy outside and let him blow the siren. Boys love to do that."

Grayson stared at her a moment then looked at me. I didn't know what to do other than shrug. I had no advice to give him. Even Keeper was taken aback. He had a part-time job at the fire department, so sirens weren't new to him. He looked at Grayson, frowning, not quite sure if he was "the boy."

Grayson opened his mouth to speak, failed to produce anything, then tried again. "Uh...yeah...Keeper, why don't we walk outside for a minute."

"But it's cold outside. Momma don't want me outside too much when it's cold."

"Keeper, it's okay. Just this one time." Mary said.

"Let's walk over to the drug store and get some hot chocolate." Grayson motioned for Keeper to follow, then closed the door behind them.

The room fell silent for an awkward moment, then Katherine said, "That is one fine looking sheriff. If I were just a little bit younger, I'd be all over that."

I jerked my head up and glared at her. I didn't know whether to be amused or threatened. Dr. Scranton had gone back to the university and, I thought, had taken my insecurity with her.

"Mother," Belinda mumbled, rolling her eyes.

Katherine paid her no attention and eased back on the couch. "My grandson, is he taken care of?"

The panic on Mary's face was real, her eyes wide with fear. "Yes," she stuttered. "He's always been taken care of."

"There's no doubt about that," I added.

"Good. You will let me know if there's ever anything he needs?"

Mary jerked her head up and down, reverting back to a scared teenager. In that moment, I couldn't blame her.

"Have you made any arrangements in case something were to happen to you? Arrangements for his care?"

"Yes," I said, jumping in and lying through my teeth. "I'm his power of attorney."

Mary shot me a panicked glance, quickly looking away as if she expected lightening to strike me down and she didn't want to witness it.

Katherine tapped her manicured nails on the tip of her cane. "I'll have a trust fund set up for him. I'll have the bank send you the account information once it's done."

Mary shook her head. "You don't have to do that. Really. He

doesn't want for anything."

"Good. He shouldn't."

Mary and I looked at one another, a million thoughts going back and forth between us. She was terrified, still, of losing her son. I could see it in her eyes. I understood now why she never told them she was pregnant. If Katherine was such a force to be reckoned with at ninety-plus years, I could image the fear she evoked in her prime.

"He doesn't know about his father, does he?" Katherine picked at a loose thread in the upholstery.

"He's never asked," Mary said in a quiet voice.

For the first time since she blew into the room, Katherine's demeanor slipped. She choked back tears, anger, whatever it was she'd held onto all these years. "If he doesn't know about his father, then it's safe to assume he doesn't know about me."

No one wanted to offer the answer, although we all knew it.

Katherine waved it off, shooing away a tear like it was a bothersome gnat. "Just as well. He probably wouldn't understand and there's no need to confuse him."

Mary didn't say anything, but the fear faded from her eyes.

Perched on the arm of the couch, Belinda finally spoke. "Mary, we were planning to take Kenny's remains back to Knoxville if that's okay with you."

Mary looked confused, trying to judge if she really had a choice. Did she even have a voice in the matter? I spoke for her. "That's thoughtful of you to ask. I'm sure Mary doesn't object. Do you, Mary?"

"No," she whispered. "I hadn't really even thought about it."

She'd been in the dark for so many years, she probably couldn't imagine being a part of the final act. She had all the closure she needed. A box of letters and a son who was the spitting image of his father.

Blayne Bell framed the shot first with his hands, then through the viewfinder. Crowded into Mary's already cluttered kitchen, Aaron dodged the sound man and maneuvered around Keeper and the lighting umbrella. He looked at Mary and gave a thumbs up. "All good?"

She nodded, smiled. She leaned into the table—the same table we'd sat at so many times before—and whispered to me, "I still don't know what I'm supposed to say."

"We're just going to talk. I'll ask a couple questions about what it is granny women do and you'll answer. Easy peasy."

"There are things we aren't supposed to talk about."

"We'll skip over those."

Aaron pulled out the other chair and sat down. Like a coach on game day. Pep talk. "We have a script if we need it, but I don't think we will. I just want you to talk. It's a conversation between friends." He talked with his hands, rolling his fingers like he was kneading dough.

I asked about the list of questions we'd prepared.

"Just remember to use the open-ended ones. Yes and no answers are matter of fact but make for a boring documentary."

"Do I need to just shut up and let her expand?" I'd never been involved in a documentary, but I'd interviewed plenty in my time. The best answers always came when I closed my mouth and opened my ears.

"Mary, can you expand?"

"My waistline expands every year."

We burst out laughing and the sound man cussed. "How am I supposed to get levels?" He barked.

We settled into giggles. I covered my mouth with my hand, trying to stifle the sound.

"Can we unplug the refrigerator? We're picking up too much white noise." The sound guy pulled his expensive-looking headset off and frowned.

Now Mary frowned. "For how long? I've got food in there I don't want to spoil."

"It won't. I promise," Aaron said, the peacekeeper.

The noise level in the tiny kitchen dropped into dead silence when the sound guy unplugged the fridge. I'd never heard the white noise before. Never knew it was there, until it was gone.

Blayne moved behind Mary, directly in front of me. "Ava, I need you to look at Mary. Don't look at me. Look right at her and don't move. You're slouching. Can you sit a little straighter?"

I pulled myself up, somewhat insulted. Rolled my shoulders back. Boobs out. Stared at Mary. "Hey, Aaron. What's next on the schedule?"

He was conferring with the sound guy then took the few steps back over to the table. "Next up is your hunter friend. The guy with the beagles."

Pudge Collins. And Tucker, the wayward beagle. Although Blayne was off framing another shot, I kept my eyes on Mary and smiled. She got her answer. She got her closure. She'd never have to wonder again if Kenny truly loved her. She had the proof. He'd told her again and again in the letters.

LYNN CHANDLER
WILLIS

Lynn Chandler Willis has worked in the corporate world, the television industry, and owned a small-town newspaper (much like Ava Logan). She's lived in North Carolina her entire life and couldn't imagine living anywhere else. Her novel, a Shamus Award finalist, *Wink of an Eye*, won the SMP/PWA Best 1st PI Novel competition, making her the first woman in a decade to win the national contest. Her debut novel, *The Rising*, won the Grace Award for Excellence in Faith-based Fiction.

The Ava Logan Mystery Series
by Lynn Chandler Willis

TELL ME NO LIES (#1)
TELL ME NO SECRETS (#2)
TELL ME YOU LOVE ME (#3)

Henery Press Mystery Books

And finally, before you go...
Here are a few other mysteries
you might enjoy:

ARTIFACT

Gigi Pandian

A Jaya Jones Treasure Hunt Mystery (#1)

Historian Jaya Jones discovers the secrets of a lost Indian treasure may be hidden in a Scottish legend from the days of the British Raj. But she's not the only one on the trail...

From San Francisco to London to the Highlands of Scotland, Jaya must evade a shadowy stalker as she follows hints from the hastily scrawled note of her dead lover to a remote archaeological dig. Helping her decipher the cryptic clues are her magician best friend, a devastatingly handsome art historian with something to hide, and a charming archaeologist running for his life.

Available at booksellers nationwide and online

Visit www.henerypress.com for details

PROTOCOL

Kathleen Valenti

A Maggie O'Malley Mystery (#1)

Freshly minted college graduate Maggie O'Malley embarks on a career fueled by professional ambition and a desire to escape the past. As a pharmaceutical researcher, she's determined to save lives from the shelter of her lab. But on her very first day she's pulled into a world of uncertainty. Reminders appear on her phone for meetings she's never scheduled with people she's never met. People who end up dead.

With help from her best friend, Maggie discovers the victims on her phone are connected to each other and her new employer. She soon unearths a treacherous plot that threatens her mission—and her life. Maggie must unlock deadly secrets to stop horrific abuses of power before death comes calling for her.

Available at booksellers nationwide and online

Visit www.henerypress.com for details

STAGING IS MURDER

Grace Topping

A Laura Bishop Mystery (#1)

Laura Bishop just nabbed her first decorating commission—staging a 19th-century mansion that hasn't been updated for decades. But when a body falls from a laundry chute and lands at Laura's feet, replacing flowered wallpaper becomes the least of her duties.

To clear her assistant of the murder and save her fledgling business, Laura's determined to find the killer. Turns out it's not as easy as renovating a manor home, especially with two handsome men complicating her mission: the police detective on the case and the real estate agent trying to save the manse from foreclosure.

Worse still, the meddling of a horoscope-guided friend, a determined grandmother, and the local funeral director could get them all killed before Laura props the first pillow.

Available at booksellers nationwide and online

Visit www.henerypress.com for details

THE SEMESTER OF OUR DISCONTENT

Cynthia Kuhn

A Lila Maclean Academic Mystery (#1)

English professor Lila Maclean is thrilled about her new job at prestigious Stonedale University, until she finds one of her colleagues dead. She soon learns that everyone, from the chancellor to the detective working the case, believes Lila—or someone she is protecting—may be responsible for the horrific event, so she assigns herself the task of identifying the killer.

Putting her scholarly skills to the test, Lila gathers evidence, but her search is complicated by an unexpected nemesis, a suspicious investigator, and an ominous secret society. Rather than earning an "A" for effort, she receives a threat featuring the mysterious emblem and must act quickly to avoid failing her assignment...and becoming the next victim.

Available at booksellers nationwide and online

Visit www.henerypress.com for details

CPSIA information can be obtained
at www.ICGtesting.com
Printed in the USA
LVHW021532150222
711208LV00010B/684

ML 02/2